Miss Aggie looked up at her friend.

"But, Eva, you know Robert's body was unrecognizable because of the acid that was thrown on him. What if it wasn't really him at all? What if the brawl was just a setup with some of his friends to help him fake his own death?" She paused and swallowed, her eyes darting around the room. "What if he's back? He always said he'd kill me someday."

Don't miss out on any of our great mysteries. Contact us at the following address for information on our newest releases and club information:

Heartsong Presents—MYSTERIES! Readers' Service
PO Box 721
Uhrichsville, OH 44683
Web site: www.heartsongmysteries.com

Or for faster action, call 1-740-922-7280.

Miss Aggie Cries Murder

A Misadventure of Miss Aggie Mystery

Frances Devine

HEARTSONG
PRESENTS
MYSTERIES

For my daughter, Sandra Gamache. See, I told you your turn would come. Love you, sweetie.

For Lisa and Shelly, because you've both finally started reading the first Miss Aggie book.

For all my angels, grandangels, and great-grandangels. I'm so blessed to have you.

Special thanks to Cedric Benoit for allowing me to mention him and his band, The Cajun Connection, in my books.

Once more, thank you, Carol, for your daily prayers.

And for my heavenly Father. Thank You for allowing me to do this.

*"For there is nothing hidden that will not
be disclosed, and nothing concealed that will not
be known or brought out into the open."*
LUKE 8:17

ISBN 978-1-60260-208-3

Scripture taken from the HOLY BIBLE, NEW INTERNATIONAL VERSION®. NIV®. Copyright © 1973, 1978, 1984 by International Bible Society. Used by permission of Zondervan. All rights reserved.

All of the characters and events in this book are fictitious. Any resemblance to actual persons, living or dead, or to actual events is purely coincidental.

Cover design: Kirk DouPonce, DogEared Design
Cover illustration: Jody Williams

Our mission is to publish and distribute inspirational products offering exceptional value and biblical encouragement to the masses.

Printed in the U.S.A.

1

They found the body at 7:09 a.m. on a hot and humid Thursday in August.

Almost seven months to the day after the Cedar Chapel Bank robbers kidnapped Miss Aggie. Just as we were getting our lives back to normal. You know that scripture—the one that says something about people saying peace, peace, but there isn't any peace? Okay, so maybe the present situation doesn't really fit, but I had begun to relax and think peace would reign for a while. Yeah, right. The calm before the storm. Ah, there I go again. My thoughts don't usually run in clichés. But then, my life doesn't usually run on a human hamster wheel, either.

I was in the basement laundry room of Cedar Lodge Boarding House, of which I'm the owner and manager. I'm the cook, too, since Corky deserted me to turn Pennington House, his and Miss Aggie's ancestral home, into a luxury hotel. He's there night and day. He even sleeps there. But I'm happy he's seeing his dream fulfilled. I'm also happy to say that a couple of the senior ladies who live here have wonderful culinary skills and are willing to use them. Oh, I'm also the housekeeper, with a little help from a couple of teenagers who come in on weekends.

Anyway, as I stood in front of the dryer, with perspiration dripping from my chin, the phone rang. Wondering who would be calling at eight in the morning, I slung the last wet towel inside, slammed the dryer door shut, and pushed the START button.

Take my word for it—don't ever run up a flight of stairs in sandals. Tripping on the top step, I fell headfirst through the door and onto the kitchen floor, where I lay in a daze.

"Victoria!" Miss Georgina Wilder's shriek knifed through my head as she rushed into the room. She came to a dead stop just in time to keep from stumbling over my feet and stared down at me, her rosebud mouth agape and silver curls awry.

"Whatever are you doing on the floor?" She shoved the cordless phone at me. "It's Aggie. Something dreadful has happened!"

I pushed up on one elbow and took the phone with my other hand. "Miss Aggie? What's wrong?"

"Get over here to the hotel. There's been a murder."

What? I reached up to rub my head and banged it instead with the phone. "Miss Aggie, what did you say?"

"I said. . ." An impatient snort bounced off my ear. "You know very well what I said. Now, hurry. Corky's away on business, and I need you." I heard a bang. Then, silence.

I sat, phone in hand, as the room revolved around me. I was getting too old for all this excitement. After all, I'd be thirty-one my next birthday.

"Victoria? Are you all right, dear?" Miss Georgina's trembling voice snapped me to my senses.

"I'm fine, Miss Georgina. Just need to let the room stop spinning." I peered up at her. Uh-oh. Panic filled her round eyes as she wrung her hands. I'd better move before she reached full-blown hysteria.

I took a deep breath and scrambled to my feet, grabbing the edge of the counter as another wave of vertigo hit me.

"Maybe you should call Dr. Stephens, dear. You don't look very well."

I patted the sweet lady's slightly plump shoulder. "No, I'm fine. Really."

"Well then, shouldn't we go? Aggie said someone's been murdered." Georgina started to scurry away even while she was still talking. "I'll get the others while you grab your keys. We'll meet you in the garage."

"Maybe I should go alone. Don't you think?"

She whirled around. The pleading expression on her face was answer enough.

Why do I bother? There was no way any of the seniors would be left behind when a mystery was in the air. Especially when one of their own was involved. "Okay, okay. Round up the gang." Ever since we rescued Miss Aggie last winter, the seniors fancy themselves sleuths. To tell the truth, I'm pretty sure they've been studying the methods of Jane Marple and Hercule Poirot. It doesn't help that they've all known me since I was born and pretty much think they have to take care of me now that Grandma and Grandpa are gone.

I hurried down the hall and into my office, groaning as I grabbed the van keys off my desk. Was Miss Aggie destined to always run headlong into trouble? No, of course not. I knew better than that. But what had she gotten herself into this time?

By the time I stepped through the kitchen door into the garage, five seniors had already piled into the van, and our monster of a dog, Buster, panted happily over the steering wheel.

"Move over, you beast." I gave him a shove through the bucket seats into the back and slid behind the wheel.

"Whose idea was it to bring Buster along?"

"His." The answer came in chorus, and I grinned. Of course it was Buster's idea. I pulled out the drive and headed down the street toward Main.

"Oh!" Miss Georgina's shrill exclamation cut through my throbbing head like an ice pick. "I wonder if Jenny would like to come along? Did anyone think to ask?"

Frank Cordell snorted. "Don't you mean 'Jeannette'?" He exaggerated the name, and a bevy of giggles answered his sarcastic tone.

"Now, don't go making fun of Jenny." Miss Evalina Swayne's reprimand merely caused more laughter to erupt. She glanced at me from the front passenger's seat, where she somehow managed to sit ramrod straight, and shook her head.

"Well, I don't know how you can all laugh and carry on like this," Miss Georgina piped up. "After all, someone's been m–m–murdered." Always the most sensitive one of the group, her stammer revealed she was nearly in tears.

I thought it time to intervene. "So. . .was Miss Simone born here in Cedar Chapel, or did she move here later?" There, gossiping about our newest boarder should keep them busy.

Martin Downey cackled. "Jenny *Simon* was born and raised here. Ran off when she was seventeen with a traveling salesman who claimed to be a Hollywood talent scout."

"No, she didn't, Martin. She left by herself. There may have been a talent scout later, though. After all, she did get into the movies." My heart warmed at Miss Georgina's softly spoken words.

There didn't seem to be an answer to that, so the van fell silent for a few seconds until Miss Jane spoke up.

"I've always thought her story was rather tragic. What with—"

I swerved as a cat ran out in front of the van. Miss Georgina screeched, and Miss Evalina held on to the dashboard.

"For heaven's sake, Georgina. Get off me," Miss Jane scolded.

"Sorry," I muttered. I headed out of town and down the blacktop that would take us to the steep, dirt road, which led to Pennington House.

"There's where we found Buster last year!" Excitement laced Miss Jane's voice.

"Buster!" Frank sputtered. "Get your tail outa my face."

"He's excited because he recognizes the place," said Miss Jane.

"He's excited because he heard his name," Martin retorted.

"You missed the turn!"Miss Georgina shrieked.

I slammed on the brakes and backed the van up then turned onto the obscure dirt road that led to Pennington House. They'd need to put a sign up when the place was ready for business. The seniors chattered as we drove up the steep hill. We arrived at the top and pulled up in front of the stately one-hundred-year-old mansion. Miss Aggie's nephew, Dane—or Corky, as we all call him—had started the renovations on their family home. They'd hoped to have it ready for the grand opening of the hotel and restaurant next summer, but a murder on the premises? Surely Miss Aggie was mistaken. At least I hoped so.

The sun glinted on the sheriff's car and Cedar Chapel's

bright red fire truck, which were parked in the wide circular drive. There was no sign of a crime team. Must not have arrived yet. I groaned at the sight of Miss Aggie standing by the porch steps nose to nose with Bob Turner. *Oh no, Miss Aggie. Don't get us into another fight with the law.* The last time, the sheriff wanted to throw me into the slammer.

Before I could put the van into park and remove my seat belt, the seniors were out of the car and making their way to Miss Aggie's side. She might be annoying at times, but she was still their friend, and this gang stuck together. Especially against Bob Turner, who they all said was "getting too big for his britches."

I grabbed Buster, who was standing by the van, staring up at me, and shoved him back inside.

"Bob Turner, you always were an idiot!"

Ouch! Did Miss Aggie really say that? I hurried over and put my arm around her shoulders.

"Now, Miss Aggie. Calm down." I cringed the moment the hasty words were out of my mouth.

I dropped my arm as Miss Aggie jerked her head around, her smooth, jet-black french twist, which I now knew was dyed, not moving an inch. Her blue eyes squinted, and she pressed her lips together tightly. She took a deep breath and glared at me as though I were a child.

"Calm down? Did you say, 'calm down,' young lady?"

"I'm sorry. I only meant because of your blood pressure, you know?"

Why am I such a coward?

I glanced at the sheriff. His face was as red as a lobster, and I didn't think it was from the sun. Cords stood out from his neck, and his fists were clenched.

"Could someone tell me what happened?" I planted myself between the sheriff and Miss Aggie before she could do further damage.

"It looks like some guy, probably a drifter, sneaked into the house and got himself locked in the tunnel by mistake. I figure he tripped and hit his head." That explained the absence of a crime team. The sheriff didn't think there had been a crime.

Miss Aggie huffed.

Sheriff Turner smirked. "Miz Brown, however, thinks someone killed him." Sarcasm dripped from his twisted mouth.

I glanced at Miss Aggie's pinched face and rigid shoulders. She looked as though she'd erupt like a volcano at any moment. And yet, I perceived something more than anger. Worry shadowed her blue eyes.

I peered at her, concern niggling at me. "Why do you think the man was murdered?"

"How would a transient know there was a tunnel there?" A strange look crossed her face, and she pressed her lips together.

"Maybe he just stumbled onto it."

"No!" She stomped her foot. "Don't be stupid. Don't you think the crooks who were holed up here last winter would have found it if it were that easy? They could have gotten away from here if they'd known about the tunnel." She shook her head. "No. A bloodstained rock was right beside his head. Someone hit him."

I didn't especially like being called stupid, but Miss Aggie had a point. "Sheriff? She could be right."

"Now you listen here, Victoria Storm. Don't you get

any ideas and start sticking your nose into police business again. You hear me?"

"Of course, Sheriff." *Although we did solve the crime for you last time.* I decided I'd better not say that, so instead, I smiled my most sincere smile and nodded.

The sheriff eyed me for a minute then scratched his head. "Well, okay. That's better."

Benjamin Grant's brand-new black and silver Avalanche pulled into the drive. His toy, I called it. He must have heard the police call over his scanner. I grinned as he got out and sauntered over to us, but when he leaned in and planted one right on my lips, I jerked away and glared at him. Okay, so we're dating and we're sort of unofficially engaged. But did that give him the right to blatantly stake his claim in public? He took a step back and chuckled. Oh. So now he was laughing at me.

"What's going on, Sheriff?"

Sheriff Turner narrowed his eyes and grunted. "Nothing to interest you, Grant. Some bum had an accident." Apparently, the sheriff wasn't ready to open up to the owner and sole reporter of the *Cedar Chapel Gazette*. Not that that would stop Benjamin.

Miss Aggie opened her mouth, and I shook my head slightly and took her arm. "Well, I guess there's no reason for us to stay here—right, Sheriff? Miss Aggie probably needs to go home and rest."

Casting a shrewd glance my way, Miss Aggie nodded in agreement.

"Nah, you don't need to hang around. If I need another statement from Miz Brown, I'll call and she can come in. But the construction crew can give me pretty much any information I need."

"Well, then. Come on, everyone." I turned and headed for the van with the seniors following.

"See you later, Ben," I threw over my shoulder.

"Wait a minute."

I sighed as Benjamin hurried after us. I never could fool him. His intent blue eyes examined my face. "You're up to something."

"What do you mean? Up to what?"

"I don't know, but I'm going with you."

"Fine. I've no idea what you're talking about, but you're more than welcome to come along with us if you like. I planned to invite you to lunch anyway."

Benjamin's eyes lit up, and he grinned. "You did?"

"Of course."

"I accept. But you might as well—" Coroner Ralph Hatcher's black sedan topped the hill and pulled into the drive. He jumped out and practically skipped over to the sheriff. Did this guy love his work or what?

Without a word, the seniors, Ben, and I watched as Sheriff Turner whispered to Ralph then took him inside.

"Well, I guess this is still my house." Miss Aggie stomped over to the wide, front porch and sat on a wicker chair. When her friends all followed, I looked at Ben and shrugged. I figured we might as well join them. Maybe the coroner could clear some things up. Ben and I sat on the top step.

We waited in silence except for an occasional sigh from Miss Aggie. Finally, Bob and Ralph came out the massive oak door. I strained to hear what they were saying, but when the sheriff saw us there, he clammed up like a. . .well, like a clam. He stalked over, ignoring everyone but me.

"You might as well go home, Victoria. There's nothing

for you to nose into here. And I'd hate to have to arrest you for obstructing justice."

Obstructing justice? By sitting on a front porch?

"But, Sheriff—"

"Now, just go on home." The sheriff's tone switched from belligerent to near cajoling. "We're removing the body. There'll be an autopsy, and if anything turns up, I'll let Dane or Miss Aggie know."

Sure he would. The gang and I piled into the van and waited while Miss Aggie pulled her car around behind us. Benjamin stood and looked uncertainly from me to the sheriff. An idea popped into my mind, and I got out of the car and walked back to Miss Aggie. Leaning in through the window, I whispered my plan then hurried back to the van where the rest of the gang were fidgeting.

As I pulled out, I glanced in my rearview mirror and saw Ben jump into his truck. When we reached a turn-around on the side of the road, I pulled over and Miss Aggie stopped smoothly behind me. Ben's mouth fell open as he whizzed by, and I chuckled at the exasperated look on his face.

Miss Georgina giggled. "Good job, Victoria."

I wasn't surprised when Ben squealed to a stop and backed up, barely squeezing the Avalanche in front of the van. I'd filled the seniors in on my idea, and they were already getting out of the vehicle.

"What are you up to?" Benjamin yelled, as he slammed the truck door.

"Shhhh." A chorus of warnings bombarded him.

"For heaven's sake, Benjamin. Be a little quieter." Miss Jane's whispered reprimand was followed by a huff from Miss Evalina.

"Sorry. What are you planning?" Ben whispered.

"Simple. We'll sneak through the woods and circle around until we're close enough to hear what they're saying."

Well, it seemed like a good idea at the time. At least we saw them bring the body bag out and put it into the ambulance before Miss Georgina sneezed and the sheriff spotted us. Then Benjamin got chewed out by Sheriff Turner instead of me. All I got was a look of disgust thrown in my direction.

Now, an hour later, I pulled the van into the drive at the lodge, leaving room for Miss Aggie to pull around me and into the garage. As everyone headed for the front door, Ben's truck stopped in front of the house. Shoot. I was hoping he'd nose around the morgue instead of coming back here. Didn't really matter, though. We might as well tell him Miss Aggie suspected murder. He'd find out anyway. I waved to him and stepped into the wide, oak-paneled foyer.

Ten minutes later, I carried a tray of iced tea into the small parlor. I smiled at Miss Simone sitting beside Miss Aggie on the sofa. Most of the time our retired diva stayed in her suite except for meals and an occasional outing.

After I'd passed around the tall, frosted glasses, I sat on a small chair in the corner while Buster plopped down on the floor beside me.

"Miss Aggie, would you care to start at the beginning and tell us why you think the dead man was murdered?"

Miss Aggie sat tapping her fingers on the sofa, a worried frown on her face.

"I think it has something to do with my husband."

Miss Jane peered at her friend. "But how could it?

What in the world do you mean? Robert's been dead for years."

Miss Aggie sighed and closed her faded blue eyes. Taking a deep breath, she opened them again and looked around the room at her old friends. She stood and began to pace, her hands knotted tightly at her side. "How can we be sure?" she whispered.

Miss Evalina stood and hurried across to her. Putting her arm around Miss Aggie's shoulders, she guided her to the sofa and pushed her gently back onto the soft cushion. "Aggie, calm down a minute. You don't know what you're saying."

Miss Aggie looked up at her friend. "But, Eva, you know Robert's body was unrecognizable because of the acid that was thrown on him. What if it wasn't really him at all? What if the brawl was just a setup with some of his friends to help him fake his own death?" She paused and swallowed, her eyes darting around the room. "What if he's back? He always said he'd kill me someday."

2

Vickie, promise me you won't do anything foolish. The sheriff is probably right about the drifter thing. Don't go riling him up."

Benjamin and I stood on the front porch. I was relieved that he'd decided to leave. I needed some time alone to think. I looked into his eyes and nodded, giving him what I hoped was a convincing smile.

He wasn't buying it. "Now, Vickie—"

The front door swung open with a bang, and Buster bounded out. Whirling around, he crouched facing the door, emitting a menacing growl from deep in his throat. Frank came through the door, struggling with an enormous covered birdcage. Miss Aggie followed, huffing and puffing, a suitcase in each hand and a sixties-style pillbox hat perched at a precarious angle on top of her head. As frantic squawks issued from beneath the cover of the cage, Buster jumped at the swinging contraption, barking at the top of his lungs.

"Hey, where are you going?" Benjamin took the heavy bags from Miss Aggie while I grabbed at the dog.

"Stop it, Buster!" I yelled, as I pulled him away from Frank and the cage.

"Jefferson City," Miss Aggie gasped between breaths. "I'm not going to wait around here and get murdered like that man in the tunnel, Robert or not. I'm going to my nephew Simon's house in Jefferson City."

"Is that Whatzit in the cage? It is, isn't it? Miss Aggie!" She knew pets were supposed to be approved before they were brought into the lodge.

"Yes, it is. And don't give me any trouble about it. I simply kept him overnight while Clyde went to the VA hospital for a checkup. You wouldn't want the silly bird to have to stay in the shop alone, would you?"

Clyde was the local pet store owner. Most of us had a love-hate relationship with his ancient parrot, Whatzit, who loved to perch above the door and screech at customers who walked in.

But how in the world had Miss Aggie managed to get that humongous parrot cage in without my seeing her? And even more astounding was the fact she'd obviously kept him quiet all night.

"So, Clyde's back home?" I asked, keeping one eye on Buster, who'd flopped down on the porch by my feet.

"I hope so. I'd hate to cart this cranky thing to Jefferson City with me. And I'm not sure what Simon's wife would say about it."

"Well. . ." *No, don't say it, don't say it.* "If Clyde's not there, I guess I can take care of Whatzit until he gets home." *I can't believe I said that.*

Miss Aggie pursed her lips and squinted at me as though considering my offer then shook her head. "No, I'm almost sure Clyde will be home by now, but if not, that I'll take him with me. Simon and Rhonda can just deal with it." She gave me an air kiss and followed Benjamin and her suitcases around to the garage. I breathed a grateful sigh of relief as Frank trailed after her with the parrot in his cage. In a moment, the men were back. Frank groaned and held his back as he went inside. As Benjamin stepped up onto the porch, Miss Aggie's new silver Lexus backed out of the driveway, bumping the curb before she drove off down the street.

Ben frowned and shook his head. "She really shouldn't be driving."

"Why not?" I scowled. "She does all right. I don't believe she's ever even had a ticket."

"Sorry, I'm sure you're right." Benjamin tweaked my chin. "I'll head on over to the morgue and see if they've discovered the cause of death or anything else I can worm out of Ralph."

"Okay, let me know what you find out. You know Sheriff Turner won't tell me anything."

"Sure. I'll see you later. That is, if the lunch invitation is still on."

"Of course, silly." I met his lips for a quick kiss, then he hopped into his truck and peeled off down the street, just missing Mrs. Miller's trash can. So, Miss Aggie shouldn't be driving, huh?

I shook my head and walked inside. The fragrance of polished wood wafted to my nostrils, and I stood for a moment inside the heavy front door and breathed a silent *thank you* to God and Grandma. I'd always loved the lodge, and I was totally surprised and thrilled when my grandmother left it to me. I couldn't understand why my parents didn't want it, but what a blessing for me they didn't. Of course, Mom had always hated it here anyway, but how could Dad be so indifferent to the ancient home, once a real hunting lodge, where he'd grown up? Oh well, if they could be indifferent to their only child. . . Sadness coursed through me, and the old familiar pang shot through my stomach. *Stop it, Victoria. You're over that.*

A whisper drifted to my ears, and I pulled myself out of the nostalgic moment and glanced around. I slipped through the door into the dining room, expecting to see

Miss Jane and Miss Georgina in one of their dramatic huddles. But it was Miss Simone who stood across the room with her back to me, murmuring into a cell phone. I was about to make my presence known, when she raised her voice.

"No!" Her agitated cry reached clearly across the room. "I won't have anything to do with this. You didn't tell me—No, I refuse."

"Miss Simone, is something wrong?" I took a step toward her.

She started and jerked around.

"Do you always spy on your guests, Miss Storm?" She snapped the phone shut and slipped it into her pocket, frowning at me, her eyes shadowed with. . .something.

"I'm sorry. I just walked in and couldn't help but overhear. I assure you, I didn't intend to listen."

"All right then." She shoved past me into the foyer and started up the stairs. At the top, she turned and glanced down at me then headed down the carpeted hall to her suite.

Now what could that be all about? I couldn't help but wonder if she were being harassed by someone. I shrugged. Oh well. I supposed if she wanted me to know what was going on, she'd tell me.

⟨⟩

"So, Benjamin, can you come up for air long enough to tell us what you found out at the morgue?" He'd been eating steadily for at least ten minutes without so much as a glance in my direction.

He grabbed his napkin and wiped his mouth. "I

thought I'd wait until after lunch. Don't want to offend anyone while they're eating."

He glanced around at the seniors and smiled.

"That's very thoughtful," Miss Evalina said, nodding her approval.

I rolled my eyes at him, and he threw an innocent grin my way. He had these elderly ladies so fooled.

"Very well. After lunch in the parlor, everyone?" I wouldn't dare exclude them. Eager nods responded, and it seemed as though everyone speeded up their eating. Everyone except Miss Evalina and Miss Simone. Miss Evalina was too much of a lady. And Miss Simone hardly ate anything anyway.

Fifteen minutes later, we were seated in the parlor. I shot Benjamin a pointed look. He grinned, just before taking a long sip of coffee. I loved Benjamin, but too often the mischievous boy who used to torment me when we were kids made an unwelcome appearance. Lately, unease about our relationship had wormed its way into my mind. I wasn't sure why. Surely his teasing shouldn't have that effect on me.

"Benjamin!" Miss Evalina sent him the schoolteacher frown she'd perfected over the last fifty years. "Stop teasing."

He set his coffee on a side table by his chair. "Sorry, Miss Eva. Okay, I'll tell you what I know, which isn't much. According to Brad, Ralph's assistant, the guy had been dead for a couple of days. He died from a heavy blow to the back of the head, and it appears Miss Aggie was right. The position of the wound ruled out an accident. Someone hit him. Hard. And apparently left him dead or dying."

The room was as silent as a tomb for a moment then

seemed to explode with questions.

"But who was he?" Miss Georgina almost squeaked in her nervousness.

"What was he doing in the tunnel?" *Like anyone could be expected to know that, Martin.*

"What did he look like? I mean his features, hair color, and things like that?" Miss Jane leaned forward, her eyes sparkling with curiosity.

From across the room, Miss Evalina nodded at Miss Jane's question and leaned forward on the sofa. "Benjamin, could they tell the man's age?"

"Yes, ma'am. They believe he was around eighty. Maybe eighty-five."

I sat, stunned. Why would someone that old be wandering around a tunnel below Pennington House? Why wasn't he sitting on a front porch somewhere, rocking and reminiscing about the good old days? And more significantly, why would anyone want to kill an old man?

A chill enveloped the room as we looked at each other in silence.

"Could it possibly be Robert Brown?" Miss Jane voiced the thought that was running through my mind.

Frank shook his head. "I just don't believe it. There were witnesses to Robert's death. And whose body did they bury, if not Robert's?"

A harsh laugh cut through the fear and dread of the room. Miss Simone stood up. "Well, if it is Robert, Aggie won't need to worry about him killing her."

Miss Jane bit her lip. "I had no idea Aggie's husband was so mean. Of course, she would have been too ashamed to tell anyone."

"You're right, she wouldn't air her dirty laundry for us

to see. But I don't know why anyone would assume the victim is Robert," Miss Evalina said. "Although the acid had disfigured him badly, there was no question at the time that it was Robert who'd been killed. The body was the same height and weight as Robert, and some personal items were found with him."

"Maybe Aggie wasn't so sure." Miss Georgina's voice crescendoed as her words came tumbling out. "I remember at the funeral and for some time afterward Aggie behaved a little bit strangely. Don't you remember? She may have had doubts she never mentioned."

Martin snorted. "Don't you think maybe she was acting strange because her husband had just been killed?"

I knew it was time to break this up before Miss Georgina got herself so scared she couldn't sleep.

"Come on, let's not imagine things." My attempted smile didn't seem to convince anyone, including myself, so I tried another tactic. "Even if it was Miss Aggie's husband in the tunnel, there's nothing for any of you to be afraid of. And personally, I doubt that's the case. There are means of identifying bodies, and I'm sure the man was identified before he was buried."

"Well, don't be too sure of that," Frank said.

Oh Frank, can't you let it go for now?

"Don't forget, this was more than forty years ago, and they weren't as advanced in criminology as they are now. DNA for instance."

"I knew it!" Miss Georgina grabbed Miss Jane's hand.

"Stop squeezing my hand. You're cutting off the circulation." Miss Jane jerked her hand loose. "But obviously that rascal Robert treated Aggie horribly. And I'm not just talking about the money he gambled away. If he really was alive all this time, I wouldn't be a bit surprised if he came back for some shady reason and someone knocked him off."

"Maybe it has something to do with the Pennington emeralds that went missing about that time." Corky stood in the doorway, holding a glass of iced tea. He lifted the glass, and his lips turned up a mocking grin. "Here's to another family mystery."

—

"I can't say as I blame Aunt Aggie for leaving today, especially after what she went through last year." Corky leaned back in his chair and raked his fingers through his tight, reddish brown curls. "She'll know she's safe with Mom and Dad."

After the seniors had all gone to bed, Corky, Benjamin, and I had gone into the kitchen for more coffee.

"But I wish she were here," Corky continued. "Maybe she remembers something that could help with the investigation. I'm surprised the sheriff let her go."

"She took off without telling him."

Corky gave a short laugh. "That's Aunt Aggie. She pretty much does what she pleases. He's not going to like it, though."

"Oh well," Benjamin said. "Turner'll know where to find her if he needs her."

Something had been puzzling me. "I'm surprised Miss Jane and the others didn't know about the missing emeralds. Especially Miss Jane, since she and Miss Aggie were such good friends."

"I think it was kept pretty quiet at the time." Corky's

forehead wrinkled as he sat in thought. "It seems my great-grandfather took the emeralds out of the safe, intending to pick one out for a lady friend. Of course, Great-Grandmama wasn't aware of this. And I doubt Aunt Aggie was either."

"But. . .Miss Aggie's father passed away before she married Robert Brown." I knew this was true from the stories Miss Georgina and Miss Jane had told me earlier in the year when we were trying to find Miss Aggie.

Corky seemed surprised. "Huh. I must have my dates mixed up. Grandfather told me so many wild stories about the Penningtons. Still, I'm almost positive he said the emeralds came up missing the same day Aunt Aggie's husband died."

I yawned. It had been a long day. "Corky, do you want to stay at the lodge tonight?"

"Thanks, but I checked into a room at the motel. Thought it best with the hours I keep."

We all said good night, and yawning again, I climbed the stairs.

—

I punched at my pillow and flopped back down, burrowing into the downy softness. Thoughts about the murder kept twirling through my head. None of this made sense. I twisted onto my side and stared through the frilly curtains of my third-floor window. Moonlight streamed in, bathing the room in a soft glow. I really needed to take the time to replace the curtains with darkening shades.

I sat up and flung my legs over the side of the bed, searching with my feet for my bedroom slippers. Wide awake, I flounced across the room and dropped into the overstuffed chair.

Something wasn't adding up here. I needed to organize my thoughts. I reached into the drawer of the side table and took out a pen and notebook. For me, organizing meant lists. This time, it would need to be a list of questions and, hopefully, answers, since I had no real suspects.

> *Victim: Who was he?*
>
> *Fact #1: Elderly man, approximately the age Robert Brown would be if he were alive.*
>
> *Fact #2: The face and body of person buried as R.B. were disfigured, making a positive identification more difficult at that time.*
>
> *Cause of Death:*
>
> *Fact #1: A blow on the back of the head with the rock?*
>
> *Fact #2: Could not have been an accident, due to position of blow.*
>
> *Motive: Possibly something to do with missing Pennington emeralds? But if they came up missing when Mr. Pennington was alive, Robert Brown wouldn't have been in the picture.*
>
> *If, on the other hand, they came up missing on the day R.B. was supposedly killed—did he fake his death and run off with the emeralds? But then, why would he have come back? Did he hide them in the tunnel? But then, why did he wait so long to try to retrieve them?*

I yawned and leaned back in my chair, my thoughts hazy and confused. I wasn't getting very far with this list.

Maybe tomorrow I could think more clearly. I placed the pen and notebook back in the drawer and went back to bed. Hopefully, I'd be able to sleep.

As I drifted off, one final thought made its way into my foggy mind. *Did Miss Aggie know more about this than she was telling?*

3

I called Miss Aggie the next morning to make sure she was all right. Well, okay, I'll admit I had another reason for calling, but I truly was concerned about the state of her nerves. However, if she had any information she hadn't disclosed, she certainly wasn't telling me. And I don't know why she got so huffy when I asked her about the missing emeralds.

"Listen, Miss Nosy," Miss Aggie'd snapped, "that's none of your business."

As though I were prying and not searching for information to solve a crime.

I stood at the kitchen counter, peeling potatoes for a casserole Miss Jane was preparing for lunch, and stewed over the unprofitable phone conversation.

"Victoria, you're mangling those potatoes." Miss Jane took the knife and eyed me with a look of concern. "What's got you so riled up?"

"Oh, nothing."

"Hmmph!"

"Well. Okay. I called Miss Aggie this morning to make sure she's all right. I happened to ask her about the emeralds, and she lambasted me good. Why would she get so mad at me for simply asking about them?"

"Mm-hm. You just happened to ask, huh?" Miss Jane sighed. "What I really don't understand is why she never told any of us." I knew she meant herself, Miss Georgina, Miss Evalina, Frank, and Martin, the gang of seniors who'd been friends all their lives. Miss Jane laid the knife on the counter and gazed out the window. "Especially me, her best friend."

I'd hoped Miss Jane had gotten over her needy devotion to Miss Aggie. She was so independent and feisty in every other way. I guess I should have known better. Lifelong habits don't die easily. I figured I'd better change the subject.

"Look, Miss Jane. Some of the leaves on that oak tree are turning. Autumn will be here before we know it."

The look she cast my way could only be called pitying.

"They're just burned up from all the heat and drought we've been having. It's way too early for fall leaves."

"Oh, of course, you're right." I didn't mind appearing stupid if it got Miss Jane's mind off what she apparently considered Miss Aggie's betrayal of their friendship.

~~~~

"Victoria, you have to do something about the murder." Miss Evalina stood in the hallway, a frown on her face.

I'd just come downstairs after working most of the afternoon on the third floor. Two more rooms stood empty, and I hoped to have them ready for occupancy before the holiday season. I'd hired professionals for the major renovations but was doing the cleaning and redecorating myself. Today I'd been staining the hardwood floors in Grandpa's library, which connected to Grandma's sitting room, and my back was feeling the strain. Most of the rooms were carpeted, but I planned to convert these two rooms into an apartment for myself and rent out the room I was using at present.

All I wanted to do was pour myself a cup of strong, hot coffee, drop my body onto a chair, and let my mind go blank for about twenty minutes. Besides, the last time Miss Evalina had told me I needed to do something, we had been catapulted into criminal activities. Still, things had turned out well, due in many respects to her level-headed suggestions.

"What did you have in mind?" I took her arm, and we walked into the kitchen together. At least I could have that coffee while we talked. I inhaled the delicious aroma of Miss Jane's favorite gourmet vanilla blend. Good, she already had it brewing. Maybe even ready to drink.

"Well, I'm sure I don't know." Miss Evalina lowered herself gingerly onto one of the kitchen chairs. "Must we sit in the kitchen? The parlor is much more comfortable."

Yes, but if I sit in the kitchen, perhaps you'll change your mind about the need to talk about the murder, and maybe I can get those twenty minutes.

"Sorry. I can't allow Miss Jane to do all the work for dinner without some help, can I?"

"Oh, that's all right, dear." Miss Jane smiled absently. "You go along to the parlor with Eva. Georgina's coming down to help shortly." Miss Jane opened the refrigerator door and began to remove ingredients, so she didn't notice the frown I threw in her direction.

I grabbed a tray, placed our coffee and the sugar and creamer on it, and followed Miss Evalina through the door and down the hallway to the small front parlor.

Obviously, I wasn't getting out of this conversation.

Miss Evalina settled herself on the end of one of the sofas, and after I'd placed the tray on the coffee table, I sat at the other end and turned to face her.

"Would you like cream and sugar?" I asked. Miss Evalina, so stable and predictable in most things, often changed the way she drank her coffee.

"No, I'll drink it black this time." She raised her cup to her lips and drank deeply, which wasn't like her usual dainty sips.

"Do you really think there's something we can do?"

She dabbed at her mouth with a napkin then set her cup and saucer on the table and turned toward me, looking me in the eye. "I know there is. I simply have no idea what."

"But what makes you think we can come up with something the sheriff hasn't already thought of?"

She hesitated before speaking. "Bob Turner has, to my surprise, turned out to be quite competent as sheriff. He is very thorough in his job when he has all the facts, but that isn't the case here."

"But we don't have all the facts, either." And I certainly had no idea how to obtain those facts.

"True. But we know some things the sheriff doesn't. We know Aggie. We know the Pennington history."

"But. . .I still don't see. . ."

Miss Evalina leaned back against the sofa and sighed. "I know you don't see, Victoria. And I don't really understand it myself. But I think if we simply take *some* sort of action, something may present itself. Perhaps a clue everyone has overlooked."

It wasn't like Miss Evalina to make decisions on feelings alone. She was the practical, levelheaded one of the group. The one who steadied us when we tended to get ahead of ourselves. I'd probably regret this, but if she felt that strongly, I wasn't about to ignore her intuition.

"All right, then we'll do something. I'm not sure what. We'll have to run this by the others and put our heads together. We don't want to make a mistake and get ourselves into trouble with Sheriff Turner."

An expression of relief washed over Miss Evalina's face, and smiling, she took a deep breath.

"Thank you, dear. Now, I'm going to lie down for a few minutes before dinner." She stood and walked out of the room, apparently leaving the problem in my hands.

I shook my head and grinned. Because I knew, when push came to shove, Miss Evalina Swayne would do whatever she could to help. I could always count on her courage and wisdom in any situation.

"Georgina!" Miss Jane's idea of a whisper rang out in the darkness. "Stop crowding me. And let go of my arm."

Her words were loud enough to notify anyone in the vicinity that intruders were present. Us. But it had been four days since the body was found, and I was hoping the sheriff hadn't left a guard at the crime scene.

Besides, the stumbling and shuffling of everyone's footsteps as we walked through the woods, after leaving the van on the road, would have alerted anyone a mile away.

"Here, Georgina, you can hang on to me." Miss Evalina held her hand out to her cousin, who gratefully grabbed on tight.

I couldn't really blame Miss Georgina for being nervous. Night sounds surrounded us. The howl of a coyote, somewhere in the distance, conjured up images of an old vampire movie I sneaked and watched when I was about eleven. I'd been kicking myself for the past ten minutes for not waiting to come here until either Corky or Benjamin was around. Benjamin wasn't answering his cell, and Corky had gone to Springfield for the night.

We plunged from the woods and onto the wide carpet of thick grass. Pennington House, standing stark and huge in the moonlight, didn't do much to dissipate the nightmare atmosphere. I almost expected to see a bat fly from the tower window. Except, of course, Pennington House didn't have a tower. Just a dark, dank, and dingy secret tunnel. I shivered. *Stop it, Victoria Storm. It's just Miss Aggie's house.*

Frank led the way across the circular drive and up the wide steps to the porch. He pulled the yellow police tape down and stepped aside to allow Jane to unlock the massive oak door.

"I hope Aggie doesn't get mad at me." Her voice trembled, and her hand shook as she turned the key.

Martin sighed. "She wouldn't have given you a key if she didn't want you to use it."

I wasn't sure Martin's reasoning would hold water if Miss Aggie did get upset with her ever-loyal friend for letting us in, but if it eased Miss Jane, I wasn't about to say a word. The alternative would have been to allow Martin to use his burglary skills to get us into the house.

The wide hallway brought back memories I didn't want to revisit. The first room on the right was where bank robbers had held us while deciding how to get rid of us. So much for our attempt to rescue a kidnapped Miss Aggie. A shiver traveled down my spine, but I couldn't tear my glance away.

Thankfully, a loud guffaw from Martin broke the spell.

"Remember that night we were locked in here? Benjamin about broke that door down before Corky produced the key. He sure has it bad for you, Victoria."

A very disapproving look from Miss Evalina brought an abrupt stop to his teasing. A good thing. I didn't want to think about my relationship with Benjamin just now, especially when I had a pretty good idea of what his reaction would be to our little escapade tonight.

"Which way to the tunnel?" I glanced from one to another of the seniors who were looking at each other in confusion. Then it dawned on me. "Don't tell me you don't know where it is?"

"Well, to be honest, we've all heard stories about the tunnel, but Aggie never would confirm or deny its existence," Miss Evalina said. "We all thought it was merely a rumor. I was as surprised as anyone when it was discovered. I'm not sure Aggie even knew it was really there."

"Yes, she did." Frank's face blazed. "I know where it is. Aggie showed me the tunnel years ago, when we were. . ."

I glanced at Miss Evalina. All eyes were on her pale face. She and Frank had been childhood sweethearts until Aggie Pennington had come between them. Frank and Aggie's romance hadn't lasted long, and Frank had eventually married someone else. But Miss Evalina had never gotten over the love of her life.

Miss Evalina cleared her throat, smiled, and openly winked at Frank. "Ah well, then lead the way, Romeo." Laughter cleared the air, and the tension dissipated.

What a gracious and spunky lady. I knew she and Frank were still in love. In fact, Frank had proposed to her a few months ago, and she'd turned him down, saying she wasn't sure she could trust him and preferred to continue a friendship, which still remained strong. Personally, I thought she was playing hard to get to teach him a lesson. And lately, they'd seemed a little more chummy than usual.

Frank grinned and held out his hand, which she took with a flourish, and they led the way down the hall to the second door on the left, just past the staircase.

"You mean it's right here in the library?" Georgina squealed, her eyes bright with surprise.

"Well, sort of." Frank walked over to what appeared to be built-in bookshelves. Removing a book from the third shelf, he reached his hand inside the shelf, and suddenly, the entire bookcase swung out. I don't know why we all gasped. The door that was revealed was exactly what we had expected to see. Frank opened the door, and we peered through. And gasped again. Because this time, we didn't see what we'd expected. Instead of a damp, dingy corridor, a carpeted hallway stretched out before us.

"This is the tunnel?" Miss Jane's voice mirrored the confusion I felt.

"This is *a* tunnel. But not *the* tunnel." Frank snapped his flashlight on, motioned for us to follow, and stepped onto the ruby-colored carpet.

My mind whirled as I followed Frank, my feet sinking into the plush floor. After a few yards, the hall made a sharp turn, and we continued down the narrow passageway. Finally, the hallway ended abruptly, and on our right stood another door. Frank turned the knob, and we entered a spacious room. A massive desk stood against one wall, and half a dozen overstuffed chairs were scattered around the room. A bar stood against another wall, and on the wall was a map.

Frank walked over to a small fireplace next to the map. He reached inside, and the fireplace swung out to reveal a plain door, which he opened.

"Here," he said, "the tunnel continues. The body was farther down, by the other entrance. Before she left last week, Aggie told me she never knew about the other entrance or that there was a tunnel behind the fireplace until the workers found it."

No wonder Miss Aggie had been so agitated the day the body was found. But why didn't she just say it was a surprise to her?

My mind whirled. Puzzled, I finally asked the question that had been swirling around in my thoughts for the past few moments. "But, Frank. What about the room?" If not for the dust and a few cobwebs, it appeared as it probably had fifty years before. Could it have been used recently? "What was the secret room for?"

Frank shrugged. "Aggie didn't know. And she wasn't about to ask her father."

When Miss Georgina and Miss Jane had told me about Aggie's family, they'd mentioned rumors that Mr. Pennington's wealth might have been acquired by less-than-honest means. *What if those rumors were true?*

4

The beam from Frank's flashlight revealed a narrow corridor. He stepped inside, and I followed. The concrete walls seemed to close in on the packed dirt floor, and my imagination conjured up a nightmare world alive with crawly things. I felt myself start to hyperventilate and concentrated on taking shorter breaths.

"What are you doing?" Frank turned and scowled.

"I need a minute."

He tapped his foot on the floor and exhaled loudly as he waited for me. Frank was usually the epitome of patience, but I suspected nerves were getting to all of us.

"Okay, I'm ready." I stepped forward.

Miss Georgina followed.

As we crept along the damp, musty corridor, I could hear heavy breathing behind me. I hoped Miss Georgina didn't panic like I had.

Darkness hung over me like a shroud, the only light coming from Frank's flashlight, straight ahead.

A muffled cry came from behind me. I grabbed my chest at the same moment Miss Georgina grabbed me from behind.

"What's wrong? Miss Georgina, what is it?" I put my arm around her and noticed she was pulling at her face.

She whimpered then gave a little laugh. "I guess it was only cobwebs."

"Everyone hold up a minute!" Miss Jane's whispered exclamation brought us up short. "I think someone's here. I heard something."

I held my breath and listened. Sure enough, it sounded like voices coming from ahead of us.

Turning, we scrambled back down the tunnel and slipped back into the room. Frank closed the door to the tunnel behind him.

"It's probably the sheriff," Frank whispered. "We should be okay here unless they heard Georgina. They probably don't know about this room. Just the tunnel and the other entrance."

"Well, won't they see the door?" Miss Jane said. I was wondering the same thing. Besides, wouldn't they have done a thorough search after the body was found? How could they not know? I had a feeling Frank was indulging in wishful thinking.

We heard footsteps in the tunnel then the muffled sound of voices. I heard a scratching sound, and the door swung open. Deputy Tom Lewis yelled and jumped back.

So much for them not knowing about the room.

"What happened?" Bob Turner's face appeared. When he saw us, he groaned.

"Hello, Sheriff. Fancy seeing you here." My voice broke, and I knew my bluff wouldn't work.

"You do know this is breaking and entering?" The deputy's stern voice couldn't cover up the fact that he was still shaking.

"No, it isn't," Miss Jane retorted. "Aggie gave me a key." She held it up.

Sheriff Turner reached as though he would take the key, but she quickly closed her fingers around it.

"Well, Miz Brody, this happens to be a crime scene, so you've still entered unlawfully."

Uh-oh. The sheriff must be mad to snap like that at Miss Jane. "And," he said, "I could haul the lot of you down to the jail and lock you up."

Miss Evalina leaned forward and looked him in the eye. "Now that would be a pretty picture for the newspaper, wouldn't it, Bob?"

"Now, Miz Swayne, don't you be too sure I won't do it." He attempted to stare into her eyes, and I almost laughed at how quickly he looked away. He was just one more of her former students who felt as though he were about to get sent to the office.

He crossed to the door leading to the library and opened it. "Okay, I want you out of here right now, and if I catch any of you near this place again, believe me, I will take you in."

We marched down the carpeted hall, through the library, and out into the foyer. As soon as we cleared the front door, Martin let out a loud guffaw.

"Did you see their faces?" He took out a white handkerchief and wiped his eyes while he continued to laugh. I wasn't laughing, though. It wasn't likely we'd be able to get into the place again, now that we'd gotten caught.

We trudged through the woods to the van and piled in. I glanced up and noticed that Frank and Miss Evalina were holding hands again. Good. Maybe Frank *was* making progress in his wooing.

"We still haven't found any clues," Martin grumbled.

He was right, and I was tempted to turn right around and try to sneak back in. "We don't know any more than we did before, except that there's a secret room."

"Odd about that room," Miss Jane said. "Why would Mr. Pennington have needed it, unless he really was mixed up in something illegal?"

"Who knows?" Miss Georgina piped up. "Maybe he just wanted a place to be alone. He loved to read, you know."

"Maybe, but there are easier ways of finding alone time than going to the trouble of digging a tunnel and building an elaborate room." Sometimes, as the saying goes, Miss Jane hit the nail right on the head.

—

It was nearly ten o'clock when we got back to the lodge. There was no sign of Miss Simone, so I assumed she'd gone to bed. I went to the kitchen and put water on for tea, and the seniors went to the front parlor.

As I was preparing the tea cart, the phone rang.

"Hi, Vick." Benjamin knew I hated it when he called me Vickie, and he had a thing for nicknames, so lately he'd shortened it to Vick, as though I'd like that better.

Irritated, I said ultrasweetly, "Hello, Benjamin. How may I help you?"

"Oops. Sorry about that. Let me start over. Hi, Victoria, love of my life."

I tried to harden myself to the laughter in his voice but couldn't keep from smiling. I felt myself loosening up. "Hi, Ben. Want to come over for tea?" With our schedules, late-night visits weren't anything unusual for Ben and me.

"I was hoping you'd ask. Be right there. 'Bye."

A tingle of anticipation ran through me. In spite of my irritation at him lately, Ben could always cheer me up. And regardless of where our relationship might be headed, tonight I needed cheering.

He arrived as I was pushing the cart into the parlor. The weather was pleasantly cool, unusual for August, so we had turned off the air conditioner and opened the parlor windows.

"Hey, a bunch of night owls," Ben teased as he saw the seniors all congregated in the parlor.

"Well, we had an adventure tonight," Miss Georgina said, her eyes bright.

"Oh? What happened?"

I groaned, trying to catch Miss Georgina's eye but to no avail. I should have warned everyone not to mention our escapade.

"We went to Pennington House," Miss Georgina said breathlessly.

"To look for clues," Miss Jane added, with a sparkle in her eyes.

Frank took the story from there. By the time he reached the part about our near arrest, Benjamin was glaring at me.

"What?" I asked, with what I hoped was a convincingly innocent smile.

"You know what. You promised me not to do anything dangerous and then went right off on another of your harebrained schemes."

Was he raising his voice to me?

"Excuse me, Benjamin Grant. Since when did you become my keeper?" I made my voice sound as indignant as possible.

"Your keeper? I never thought of myself as your keeper, but maybe you need one. What you did was dangerous, and you know it." He paused and brushed his hair back from his eyes, a gesture he often used when he was frustrated.

I felt a twinge of regret but not enough to back down. "It wasn't dangerous, Ben," I said from between clenched teeth.

"Not dangerous? Not dangerous? How about a murdered man being found there? Remember that?" Now why did he have to bring that up?

"Well, it's not dangerous now. The murderer isn't coming back to the scene of his crime when he knows the police will be all over the place." Did I really believe that? "And I'd never put the gang in danger. You know that." But had I actually done that very thing?

"Victoria, I don't want you near that house again. Do you hear me?"

"I hear you, all right. And now, you hear me. Don't tell me what I can or can't do."

By now, our voices were raised, and I noticed Miss Evalina lowering the front window.

We stood nose to nose, trying to stare each other down. Benjamin turned and stormed out of the room. I heard the front door close. Or was that a slam?

I stood for a moment, feeling sick inside, secretly wishing Benjamin would come back. This was the first time I'd lost my temper in a long time. But he shouldn't have been so bossy. So much for cheering me up.

With resolve, I pushed the guilt aside and took a deep breath. I sat and picked up my tea, avoiding all the eyes that I knew were looking straight at me.

"My, my."

"Shh. Georgina, hush." Bless Miss Evalina. She knew me so well. She patted Georgina's arm gently.

"I'm sorry, folks." And I meant it. I knew how it upset them when Ben and I argued. I thought we'd overcome that, but I guessed not. We seemed to bring out the worst in each other. Maybe my doubts about us had basis in reality. Maybe we really weren't meant to be together.

I blinked back the tears that threatened to escape my eyes. Why couldn't I have just admitted it was foolish for us to sneak into Pennington House?

One by one, the seniors said good night and went upstairs. Miss Evalina was the only one who remained.

Silently, we cleared away the tea things and walked upstairs to her room. She gave me a hug before she said good night.

When I reached Miss Simone's suite, I wondered if I should check to make sure she was settled in for the night. I didn't like to go to bed until all the boarders were accounted for. Not wanting to startle her, I tapped softly on the door then reached for the old-fashioned brass knob and turned, but it was locked. Good. I turned away and headed up to my third-floor room.

I crawled between cool sheets and pulled the lightweight down blanket up to my chin. I closed my eyes, intending to pray, but immediately thought of Benjamin. Determined not to think of him, I forced my thoughts onto something else—the secret room with its ruby red carpet. Or was that bloodred?

I groaned. Ben was right. I'd not only put myself in danger but the seniors as well. Guilt rose up in me, and I slipped out from under the covers and onto my knees.

After a restless night, I showered and came downstairs to find Miss Jane in the kitchen placing bacon on the stovetop grill. From the heavenly aroma that filled the room, I knew there were biscuits in the oven. She loved to prepare meals, and I'd given up arguing about it. Hopefully, someone would soon respond to my ad for a cook.

"Thank you so much, Miss Jane. What would you like me to do to help?"

"Everything's about done." She smiled and motioned to the coffeepot. "Have a cup of coffee. Then you can help me take everything to the dining room."

I didn't need any urging. My duties for the day would begin soon enough. I sat at the kitchen table and drank my coffee while Miss Jane chatted about our adventures of the night before.

"We handled it wrong, you know. Someone should have been on guard near the front door. We could have sneaked out the back before they got there. The sheriff would never have caught us."

Miss Jane loved excitement, and we'd been partners in investigating crime before. Once, it had just been the two of us. She'd managed to get important information from a witness before he realized what he'd said. I almost laughed aloud at the memory of the bank manager's face when he realized he'd been tricked. He'd been a good sport about it, but he showed us the door pretty fast after that.

"You're right. We should have thought of that." Hmm. I wondered if there was any way we could get back in. Guilt rose up inside me. Hadn't I just admitted to God and myself last night that our little adventure had been foolish?

"Do you think we could get back in, somehow?" Amazing how often Miss Jane's thoughts echoed my own.

"Better not try it, I guess." But even as I said the words, my thoughts were arguing, *Why not? We'd be more careful this time.*

Miss Jane and I set the food up on the buffet in the dining room. I made a few last-minute adjustments to the table just as the rest of the seniors came trailing in. I couldn't help observing that Frank and Miss Evalina walked in together, a little behind the others. She was laughing, and he was staring down at her with an adoring expression on his face. Could those two have come to an understanding without any of us knowing it? *Mind your own business, Victoria.*

"Does anyone need a ride to the senior center?" I asked between bites.

"I think we're all going, so we can ride together." Miss Jane loved to drive as many passengers as possible in her ancient black Cadillac.

"I'm not," Miss Simone said. "I have an appointment. Anyway, the food at the center is atrocious."

"Do you need a ride to your appointment?" Miss Simone had her own car, but I felt I needed to offer. Sometimes she preferred to be shuttled to wherever she was going.

"No." Okay, that was short but emphatic.

"But I appreciate the offer." A weak smile flickered over her face and died. Miss Simone had been rather abrupt and unfriendly lately. Ever since I'd walked in on her rather disturbing phone conversation.

After the boarders had all left the lodge, I planned my day. I needed to take Buster for his grooming sometime today, but I decided to go to the bank first. I'd only gone a couple of blocks when I noticed the van steered strangely, sort of veering to the left. I made a mental note to stop by Larry's Auto Repair before I went home.

Phoebe Sullivan, a teller at the bank, greeted me, and

we chatted while I made my deposit. Well, she chatted while I listened. Corky, Corky, Corky. Couldn't the girl talk about anything else? Phoebe and I were fast becoming best friends. Since I'd inherited the lodge and moved here permanently from Dallas, I'd been so busy I hadn't really tried to pursue friendships with women near my age. The girls I'd palled around with during summers and holidays here in Cedar Chapel had either married or moved away.

I had Benjamin. And I had the seniors. So until recently, I hadn't really sensed a need for more until Corky started bringing Phoebe around and I got to know her. We clicked. I wasn't sure why. She was a few years younger than I, and we were almost total opposites in personality, but it didn't seem to matter. Phoebe and I had become friends. But I wasn't in the mood to hear about someone else's romance since mine wasn't going so well. Feeling a little guilty, I responded with as much enthusiasm as I could. After all, it wasn't her fault Benjamin and I had argued. But I'd bet Corky didn't try to control her movements. Of course, I had to admit, Phoebe wasn't the type to put herself in dangerous situations. But I hadn't really been in any danger at Pennington House. Had I? I sighed, tired of my constant mental debates. I placed a few things in my safety-deposit box, returned to the lobby, waved to Phoebe, and left.

As I walked the half block to the van, I did a double take at the man getting out of the SUV parked next to mine. He was handsome to the nth degree, with dark hair blowing across his rugged forehead and intense blue eyes that were looking straight at me. I'd seen him before. I knew I had. But where?

A slight smile appeared on his chiseled face, and

my stomach lurched. Suddenly I knew why he seemed familiar. He was the hero on every Lifetime movie I'd ever seen.

He winked as I stood like a statue watching him walk past me. With my face flaming, I shook myself and got into the van. *The very nerve of the guy.*

5

I stood outside Larry's garage wondering what to do, now that the van was out of commission for a couple of days. I could walk home before it got too hot. That would be the smart course of action. One good thing about living in a small town was that everywhere was within walking distance. Yes, I should really go on home, get some receipts and things together for my accountant, maybe continue to work on the third-floor suite. Brushing the idea aside like a piece of lint, I started walking back toward the square. I'd grab a cup of coffee at Perkins' Café first and catch up on the local news. I'd have to ask Miss Jane to drive me to Clyde's store for Buster's grooming, but she wouldn't be back at the lodge until at least one o'clock.

"Well, look what the cat drug in." Hannah, the owner of the town's locally famous down-home café, had a lot of colorful phrases, most of them as outdated as the one she'd just slung at me with a wide grin. Sometimes she was a little too friendly and a lot too inquiring, but the whole town just loved her to pieces.

"Hi, Hannah. It has been awhile, hasn't it?" I started to sit at the counter then changed my mind and headed for a booth in the back. There, I could listen to the café chat without getting pulled into a conversation. Not that I was antisocial. Most of the time I loved to talk to the locals, but today, I had too much on my mind. Anyway, I hoped I could avoid questions about Benjamin this morning.

"So, where's that good-looking Benjamin Grant today?" Hannah slapped a menu on the table and turned the coffee cup over. She glanced at me and grinned as she poured.

So much for wishful thinking. "I haven't talked to him this morning." I handed the menu back. "Just the coffee, thanks, Hannah."

"Oh, honey, are you sure? You look a little hungry to me." She leaned over and peered into my face.

Everyone looked hungry to Hannah. She was on a constant crusade to feed the world with her famous home-style cooking. And it couldn't be denied, she was a great cook. Probably the best in the county.

"Don't say that to Miss Jane," I said with a chuckle. "She made hot biscuits and gravy, bacon and eggs, and oatmeal with raisins for breakfast. And I'm afraid I tried a little of everything." I grinned at the disappointed look on Hannah's face and added, "Maybe I'll stop in for lunch if I'm still out and about."

"Okay. Good. You do that. And be sure to try the chicken-fried steak. I'm making cream gravy to go with it." She waved and walked away with menu and coffeepot in hand, heading for the latest arrival, Mr. Samson, retired mailman and friend to all.

I stirred cream and sugar into my coffee, thinking wistfully of Miss Jane's vanilla blend. But the hot liquid was soothing, and I leaned back and relaxed. I hoped to be able to concentrate on the mystery at hand. After all, we could have a murderer running loose in Cedar Chapel. Miss Aggie certainly seemed to think so. And anyway, how dare anyone commit a murder on Miss Aggie's property when she and Corky were trying so hard to get Pennington House ready for business? Of course, the sheriff might have everything under control and surprise us with an arrest at any moment, but I had no intention of waiting around for that improbability.

Could it be merely a coincidence that the murder had occurred at Pennington House? After all, it was deserted and isolated. A perfect place to commit a crime. Perhaps the victim *had* been a transient and was killed by a companion for some reason. An argument, maybe. Even over food or whiskey or something of the sort.

I rummaged in my purse for a pen and took a napkin from the dispenser.

1. *Was there alcohol in the victim's blood?*

2. *Was there something significant missing from the victim's body? Such as his shoes. Did vagrants kill for shoes?*

I looked at the short list and tore it up, feeling foolish. This was getting me nowhere. I stuffed the torn napkin into my purse. If there were any clues, I hadn't found them. I wondered if the sheriff had. I sat and tapped my pen against the table, wondering how I could get information out of Bob Turner. Or maybe Tom Lewis. Maybe I'd just saunter on over to the courthouse and snoop around a little. With resolution, I stood and headed for the register.

"Well, well, Victoria Storm. I didn't see you over there." Mr. Samson had taught me to swim the summer I turned eight.

"Hi, there. How are you?" I said, smiling at him as I handed a five-dollar bill to the teenage girl behind the counter.

"Doin' good, doin' good. How's Benjamin?" I sighed. I should have known I couldn't avoid talking about

Benjamin. Especially to Mr. Samson. He'd also tried to teach Benjamin how to swim the same summer he taught me, but Ben was too busy splashing water on me to learn very much.

"He's fine, Mr. Samson. He swims really well, now."

Mr. Samson looked puzzled for a moment, then he roared with laughter as he realized what I was referring to. I was about to say good-bye, when he went into a fit of coughing. I pounded him on the back until he sputtered and caught his breath. Mr. Samson was getting old. He must be in his eighties now.

The bell over the door jangled, and I looked up. My heart thumped wildly, and I swallowed hard as the "Lifetime hero" walked through the door.

He headed straight for me. I smiled, waiting for him to speak.

"Hello there, Mr. Samson." Okay, so he wasn't heading for me, after all.

"Trent. Glad you came in. Have you met Victoria Storm?" Mr. Samson's face was still a little red from the coughing spell.

The tall, dark stranger turned toward me with an amused look in his eyes. Apparently, he'd noticed my reaction to him earlier, just as I'd feared. "No, I don't believe I've had the pleasure."

"Victoria, this is Trent Stewart. He's a writer, bought the old Rankin cabin several months ago."

"Welcome to Cedar Chapel, Mr. Stewart." I offered my hand. "What do you write?"

"Articles," he said, taking my hand. "Mostly hunting and fishing. But I'm attempting a novel. Do you like mysteries, Miss Storm?"

"Yes, I love mysteries."

"I thought so. You look like a mystery woman to me." He smiled, and his eyes seemed to smolder.

Was the room getting warmer? Resisting the urge to fan my face, I cleared my throat and slipped my hand from his.

"Well, it was nice meeting you. I really must go." I started to turn away.

"Wait, I have a favor to ask."

A favor? Of me? This gorgeous hunk needed a favor from me?

"Yes?" Did my voice tremble? Surely not.

"Actually, I'm trying to get acquainted with all my new neighbors. It's a little lonely being a stranger in a small town."

"Yes, I'm sure it is, Mr. Stewart. What can I do for you?" By this time, I'd pulled myself together and was breathing almost normally.

"I hope you won't consider this rude, when we've just met, but would you consider an invitation to dinner?" He smiled, and the teasing was gone from his eyes.

Maybe he really was lonely.

"Oh, uh, I don't know," I mumbled. "I'll have to think about it."

"Of course. Could I call you in a few days for your answer?"

I gulped. Darn it, Victoria, shape up and stop behaving like a schoolgirl.

"I suppose that would be all right. I'm in the phone book. Cedar Lodge Boarding House."

Somehow, I managed to get out the door without making a fool of myself. I hoped.

I was almost home when I remembered Benjamin. Guilt riddled me. How could I have forgotten Ben? Was it a sign of some kind? Was our relationship slipping away?

—

Buster toppled onto the Cadillac's back floorboard as Miss Jane careened around the corner. This was the third time he'd fallen, and I noticed he didn't bother scrambling back onto the seat this time. I was holding onto the edge of the front passenger seat and wishing I could join him back there.

Somehow, Miss Jane managed to park at a perfect angle in front of Clyde's pet shop.

I got out and opened the back door for Buster. My legs were shaky, and I took a deep breath to calm down. Most of the time, I could handle Miss Jane's driving, but today, I was feeling emotionally drained and didn't need the roller-coaster ride.

Buster bounded out of the car then noticed where we were and tried to scramble back in. Like he remembered his last visit here. Could he? It was months ago.

"Come on, Buster, you're not getting a shot." I clipped his leash onto his collar and tugged.

Clyde wasn't a vet and probably shouldn't be giving shots in his pet store, but it saved a drive all the way to Branson, so most of the locals conveniently forgot he wasn't licensed. A twinge of guilt clutched at me. I wasn't sure of the legality and hadn't asked. I made an inward decision to find out before Buster's next shots were due.

"Hello. Hello. Whaddya want? Whaddya want?" Startled, I dropped Buster's leash. The screeching words came from the back of the shop where Whatzit sat in his enormous cage. At least he wasn't flying around the place. Buster barked and headed for a cage where two Siamese cats sat licking their paws. They snarled, the hair on their backs standing on end, and he barked louder.

"Buster! Stop that!" He ducked his head and slunk over to Miss Jane, who grabbed his leash. One would think she beat him. I suspected he was actually afraid of the cats, caged or not.

Clyde Foster came from the back and frowned at us. I'd been afraid of him when I was a little girl, and that fear still clung to me. His gruff voice and the mean look on his face would have frightened any child, but it was time I outgrew it.

"Hello, Mr. Foster. I've brought Buster for his grooming. Just trim him a little, okay?

"You mean now?" The frown deepened, and a chill washed over me.

"Yes, sir. I made the appointment last week."

"Bring him back, then," he growled, heading for the back room. Miss Jane handed me Buster's leash, and we followed Clyde as instructed.

For the life of me, I couldn't understand how Miss Aggie could tolerate this man. But apparently they'd been friends for years. Maybe there was a redeeming quality about him I was missing. Covertly, I examined his face while he was grooming Buster. The perpetual frown seemed menacing. I wondered: *Was it stretching things to consider the possibility of Clyde being involved in the murder at Pennington House? Don't let your imagination carry you too far, Victoria.* Still. . .

"Mr. Foster, what do you think about the murder at

Pennington House?" I peered closely to see if his expression changed. It didn't.

"No business of mine," he muttered. "I don't stick my nose into things that don't concern me." He threw a baleful glance at me. "Not like some I could name."

Miss Jane poked me with her elbow before I could retort. She shook her head at me. I took her silent advice and kept quiet.

We left the shop a few minutes later, Buster prancing with joy to be free. When I opened the car door, he jumped in without hesitation.

After I'd buckled up, I turned to Miss Jane, who was starting the car. "Why'd you stop me from talking in there? He called me nosy."

She concentrated on backing into the street. Driving away, she glanced at me. "It doesn't pay to get on Clyde's bad side."

"What do you mean?" My heart pounded. Maybe there was some validity to my lifelong fear.

"Clyde was never part of our group of friends. He was a few years older. When we were kids, we didn't dare say or do anything to displease him. He could be cruel." She stopped, a pained look on her face.

"But then, why would Miss Aggie be so friendly with him?"

She sighed and shook her head. "I don't think Aggie ever knew how mean he was. You see, he was always on his good behavior with her. I suppose he was afraid of her father and brother."

Hmm. Something new to think about. Should I consider Clyde a suspect? Or was I allowing my childhood aversion to him to cloud my judgment? It couldn't hurt anything to consider him a *possible* suspect.

"Let's go sleuthing." I grinned across at her.

"I thought you'd never ask." Her face glowed with excitement. "What shall we do?"

"First, let's talk to Sheriff Turner and see if we can find out what he's up to." I looked at her and grinned conspiratorially. "He might get mad at us. Probably will. Are you game?" As if I didn't know the answer.

"Ha. Bob Turner doesn't scare me." She headed toward the square and screeched to a stop in front of the courthouse.

Out of compassion for Buster, Miss Jane left the air on then locked the car doors so no one could steal him. As if anyone but us would want him. We could hear him barking with displeasure until we entered the building.

We walked into the sheriff's department and were greeted by Tom Lewis's expression of dread. For some reason, we always seemed to give him indigestion.

"Miz Brody, Victoria."

"Tom, dear, how are you?" Miss Jane's voice rang with sincerity.

"Fine, Miss Jane. And you?" I bit my lip to keep from laughing at the look of suspicion he darted at her.

"Why, I'm doing very well, thank you." She smiled sweetly.

"What can I do to help you, ma'am?"

"Oh, we just need to see Sheriff Turner for a moment. Is he in?"

"I don't think he can see you right now, but I'll check."

"You do that, dear. We'll just wait right here."

Tom slipped out of his chair and scurried to the sheriff's office, darting glances back to make sure we weren't following. I couldn't really blame him. It wouldn't be the first time. I knew we should be ashamed of the hard time we gave the deputy. But we'd probably never get in to see the sheriff, otherwise.

Surprisingly, the sheriff agreed to see us. We sat in chairs across from him, and he smiled across his desk at us, which made me wonder what was going on.

"Good morning, Miz Brody, Victoria. What can I do for you?" He tapped a pencil on his desk, a good indication that he wasn't as relaxed as he seemed.

"Good morning, Bob." Miss Jane beamed at him. "We thought you might want to tell us if you've found any leads to the person who killed that poor man at Aggie's house."

"Well, no, I haven't, ma'am." He seemed to tense up. "But I'm sure we will soon."

I cleared my throat and leaned forward. A guarded look crossed the sheriff's face.

"Sheriff, have you investigated Clyde Foster, by any chance?" I asked.

The sheriff's face registered mixed emotions. Relief, amusement, satisfaction. Immediately, I knew. Something was going on. And I'd asked the wrong question.

I fluffed my pillow for the hundredth time and flopped over on my side. Closing my eyes again, I attempted to empty my mind of the myriad thoughts that insisted on repeating over and over in my head. After ten more minutes of tossing and turning, I sat up. This was ridiculous. If I wasn't going to fall asleep, I might as well read.

Pillows cushioned behind my back, I reached over and turned on my bedside lamp then picked up the thriller I was currently reading. After two paragraphs, I realized the story wasn't exactly conducive to sleep, so I laid it aside and got up. Maybe a cup of tea would help.

The moonlight filtered through the lacy curtains on the front door's tall, narrow side windows, faintly illuminating the stairway, so I didn't bother to switch on a light as I tiptoed down the steps. No sense waking up anyone else.

Just as I reached the bottom of the stairs, a sound caught my attention. I paused a moment, listening. The sound seemed to be coming from the great room. A faint sob.

I glided quickly across the foyer and stood in the open doorway. The great room, the original hunting lodge built by one of my ancestors several hundred years ago, yawned before me like a vast cavern of darkness. I felt on the wall for the light-switch panel and flipped the switch up.

The small lights on each side of the fireplace came on, revealing a startled Miss Simone. She sat huddled on one of the sofas, tears staining her face.

"Oh. Victoria. I didn't hear you approaching." Her

face was pinched, and she bit her bottom lip.

I hurried over and sat beside her. "I heard a noise and came to investigate. Are you all right?"

"Yes, of course I am," she snapped. "I came down for a glass of water and got a little dizzy. I just slipped in here to sit down for a moment." She stood up, and I noticed her hands trembled. "I'm fine now. I'm going up to bed. Good night."

She tromped out of the room and up the stairs.

I sat, puzzled and frustrated. What was it with Jeannette Simone? She'd called me three months ago, inquiring about the accommodations. Six weeks later, she'd moved into a newly renovated and fancied-up suite. My old second-floor apartment. Since then, she'd been reserved and kept mostly to herself, but her behavior hadn't been out of the ordinary. Until recently. About the same time the murder took place.

A chill ran through me, and I shivered. Could there possibly be a connection? I knew Miss Simone grew up in Cedar Chapel. Had she had connections with Pennington House? Could she know something she wasn't telling?

I went to the kitchen and put the kettle on. Suddenly, a memory seemed to slice through my confusion. The day the body was found, when we were driving to Pennington House, Miss Jane had started to say something about Miss Simone and was somehow interrupted. I wondered what it could have been. I'd ask Miss Jane the first chance I had.

When I got back to my room, I set the tea tray on the table by my chair and got my notebook out.

Beneath my other entries, I wrote:

Possible Suspects:

Jeannette Simone. Find out if there is anything

in her past to shed light on her actions.
Keep an eye on her activities and try to find
out who she sees, if anyone, outside the lodge.
Talk to Miss Jane.

I chewed on the end of my pen as I read over the entry. Was my imagination running away with me? Back when Miss Aggie was missing, I'd come up with some pretty bizarre theories, including adding Frank, Corky, and Miss Evalina to my list of suspects at one time or another. But Jeannette Simone was practically a stranger to me. And after all, she was living here in my home and in the same house with my friends. If there was any chance at all that she was involved in anything underhanded, I needed to know.

I put the notebook and pen into the drawer and, yawning, went back to bed. It was nearly midnight, and I breathed a prayer that sleep would be waiting to claim me.

Apparently, my prayer was not only heard but answered with a resounding "yes." I woke up when my alarm went off, stretched, and jumped out of bed refreshed and eager to face the day and whatever it held.

I practically skipped downstairs and found Miss Jane scampering about in the kitchen, ahead of me, as usual.

"Miss Jane. Did I ever tell you what a gift you are?"

"Yes, I believe you have. A number of times. But I don't mind hearing it again." She giggled and pulled a pan of biscuits out of the oven.

By the time the rest of the crew arrived in the dining

room, the table and buffet were ready.

Miss Georgina bumped her chair, nearly knocking it over as she took her place. Startled, she then almost dropped her full plate.

Martin guffawed. "Whatsa matter, Georgina? Nervous, 'cause you're gonna see your boyfriend today?"

The victim of his teasing turned red and ducked her head.

"Martin Downey, you leave Georgina alone. Right now. Do you hear me?" Miss Jane glared at Martin as she sat at the table.

Determined to head off an argument, I intervened. "Miss Evalina, would you say grace, please?"

The seniors had been planning a trip to Silver Dollar City for weeks, and everyone knew Miss Georgina had a crush on Cedric Benoit, the handsome and talented leader of The Cajun Connection. She was old enough to be his mother, and he was married to boot, but oh well. She could dream. I often thought the sweet maiden lady still saw herself as a young girl. And why not?

Miss Evalina said "Amen," and everyone dug in with gusto.

"It's too bad the van is out of service," Miss Jane said, between bites. "It would be more fun if we could all go in one vehicle."

"Yeah." Frank grunted and then smiled at Miss Evalina.

It was midmorning when the men piled into Frank's truck and the ladies into Miss Jane's Cadillac. I waved as they pulled away, relieved they'd be gone for the day. They had been hinting around that we needed to get busy solving the crime. But after I realized I could have put them in danger when we went to the tunnel, I didn't want to involve them, so I hadn't even shown them my suspect list.

Actually, I found myself wishing I had time to go with them and determined to make the trip with them soon. They always went to Branson several times during the open season. The Christmas festival, which began in early November, was my favorite. But that was a long time off.

I was supposed to interview a potential cook at 10:30, so I decided to put off cleaning until afternoon.

At 10:30 sharp, the doorbell rang. The woman who stood on the porch was tall and big-boned. Her hair was tied back in a bandanna, and brown eyes squinted at me from beneath her hooded brow. All in all, she looked like Ma in the old Ma and Pa Kettle movies that Martin sometimes watched.

"Miz Storm?"

"Yes, I'm Victoria Storm."

"M' name's Mabel Carey. I'm here to apply for the cooking job."

The gruff but kind tone of her voice pretty much won me over, and I was almost ready to offer her the job on the spot. However, I thought an interview was probably the wiser course, so I smiled and invited her in. We sat in the front parlor.

"What experience have you had, Mrs. Carey?"

She grinned. "Raised eleven young'uns. And they never had any complaints about my cooking."

"I see. Have you had any experience outside your home?" Home cooking was great. But children always like their mothers' cooking, don't they?

"No'm, never did work outside my own household. But I can cook—just about anything you want to eat."

I groaned inwardly as a worried look crossed her face. I always hated turning anyone down.

"Can you tell me some of the things you cook, Mrs. Carey?"

"Why, sure. Mostly my man and young'uns liked fried chicken, pork chops and sauerkraut, and all that stuff. But a few years ago, I got aholt of a cookbook my niece sent me and started branchin' out. Chicken *cordon bleu*, baked Alaska, and all that fancy stuff." She laughed. "You should've seen them near-grownup young'uns tear into that stuff. Now, when they come home, they want fried chicken and baked Alaska. Ain't that a combination?"

That was good enough for me. We discussed salary, the hours I expected her to work, then days off. That's when I discovered she was recently widowed.

"Yeah, Tom was as good a man as any. Always took right good care of me and the family." Sadness crossed her face momentarily. "But he wasn't ever able to put anything back with all them mouths to feed and backs to clothe. That's okay, though. The house is free and clear, and it won't hurt me none to have this job to take care of other stuff. That is, if you hire me. If not, I'd better be trottin' on down the road and try somewhere's else."

"Mrs. Carey, I most certainly will hire you. If you want the job, it's yours."

Her face brightened. "Thank you kindly, Miz Storm. But I'd be pleased if you'd call me Mabel."

"Okay with me, if you'll call me Victoria." I offered my hand, and she grinned and clutched it in hers.

After Mabel left, with a promise to be back the next morning at six, I went upstairs, got my notebook and pen, and went back downstairs. I'd decided to walk over to the Mocha Java for lunch. I was in the mood for an oriental salad, and theirs was scrumptious. The third-floor job would still be here when I was ready to tackle it. I'd look over the list while I ate. Maybe something new would occur to me. Sure, Victoria. Wishful thinking.

The lunch crowd hadn't arrived yet. That was one good thing about a small town. Everyone went to lunch at noon. Not a minute before. That suited me fine. I wasn't in the mood for neighborly conversation today.

I sat at a table in the corner with my salad and a Chai tea. After I'd eaten, I looked at the list. And looked again. Nothing jumped out at me. Nothing shouted, *Here's a clue, Victoria.*

I'd forgotten to add Clyde's name to the list so, glad to have something to do, I scribbled it in. Did I really think Clyde could have something to do with the murdered man? Or did I designate him a suspect because I had a lifelong aversion to him? He'd scared me half to death when I was a kid, and he knew it. Seemed to relish it. But was that any reason to think he'd kill someone? Maybe I should mark his name off the list. I peered at it, my pen poised to strike through it. Nah. It stayed.

I added a couple of questions beneath Miss Simone's name.

Why would a wealthy, retired actress choose to return to Cedar Chapel?

Why would a wealthy, retired actress choose to live at the lodge?

That had been worrying around in my head for a while, but now, I decided to examine it. It really was rather strange. The lodge was comfortable and quaint, but there was nothing posh about it. Except of course, for Miss Simone's suite.

"Victoria, is that you?"

Oh no. It was my next-door neighbor, Mrs. Miller. The busiest busybody in Cedar Chapel. She'd been worming secrets from me since I was four years old. Or maybe even before that. I couldn't remember back any further.

"Hello, Mrs. Miller. So nice to see you." *Victoria, you're such a liar. But Grandma taught me to respect my elders. Yeah? So what? You're still a liar.* Why did I carry on an inner conversation with myself every time I saw Mrs. Miller?

"I noticed the whole gang leaving this morning. And I didn't see them at the senior center when I stopped by." She sat down across from me and gave me a questioning look.

"They went to Silver Dollar City."

"Oh." She frowned. "Well, they might have invited me to go along."

"Do you like it there?" I hoped they hadn't deliberately snubbed her, although I couldn't blame them if they had.

"Well, not really. There's so much walking. It's hard to get around with all those hills. I have arthritis, you know."

"Yes, ma'am." But so did most of my elderly boarders. "Well, they probably knew you wouldn't be able to manage it. Otherwise, I'm sure they'd have asked you to go with them." There I went again. Couldn't I figure out a way to be nice without being untruthful?

She gave me a sour look. "Yeah, well."

I started gathering my writing tools together. It was time to make my escape.

Mrs. Miller laid her hand on my arm. I groaned. I should have known I wouldn't get off that easily.

"How are things going with Jenny Simon?"

"Uh, fine. Why?" I'd probably be sorry I asked.

"Oh. Well. I just wondered. All your boarders are such good friends and all. She must stick out like a sore thumb."

My invisible antenna perked up. Maybe this time, I'd be the one getting information from Mrs. Miller.

"Why would you think that? Do you mean they have something against Miss Simone?"

"Oh no, dear. I'm sure they don't. Anyway, how would I know if they did? Jenny Simon, as she was known before she changed her name, moved away before I came here as a bride."

I must have looked puzzled. Suddenly, she got that Cheshire cat look. As though she were ready to lick her whiskers in anticipation.

"Well, of course, I did hear rumors. But you can't believe everything you hear. And I wouldn't want to repeat gossip."

Okay, if she had information about Miss Simone, I was going to get it out of her if it took all day.

"No, of course not. Still, if you know of anything that could cause potential trouble at the lodge, I'd appreciate it if you'd clue me in."

"Well, in that case, as much as I hate to repeat it. . . they say, you know, that before she became a star, Jenny Simon was Forrest Pennington's mistress. And that he threw her over for another woman."

Mabel showed up at six the next morning. Miss Jane offered to assist her for a day or two until she learned the ropes, and I gladly accepted the offer. The day went smoothly, with the two women getting along well in spite of personality and background differences. By the end of the day, even Miss Jane had to admit the new cook didn't need her instructions or help any longer, so with obvious reluctance, she relinquished her duties in the kitchen to Mabel.

I caught her as she came out into the foyer, looking a little bit despondent. Maybe I could cheer her up.

"Miss Jane, do you think you could take over for Mabel on her day off?"

She nodded, silently. Okay, something else was wrong. "Are you all right?"

She sighed. "I thought they'd have found the murderer by now. It's been a week today."

I inhaled and decided she needed some action. After all, the seniors were all adults with sound minds. I had no right to treat them like children. And Miss Jane, of all of them, had the most adventurous nature. "You're right. So you and I are going to try to solve this thing."

"We are?" A glimmer of excitement washed over her face.

"Yes. I have some things to talk over with you and a list of possible suspects to show you. But first, I think you can help with some information."

"What is it?"

"Look, I don't want the whole clan involved at this point, not until I get a few things figured out. Could I talk to you privately, please?"

Curiosity crossed her face, and she followed me into the great hall where we weren't as likely to be disturbed.

I closed the heavy oak door, and we sat in the wing chairs by the curved, triple windows on the front wall.

"What is it, dear?" Miss Jane whispered. Then she added with a giggle, "I don't suppose we need to whisper in here, do we?"

"I shouldn't think so," I agreed, wondering where to begin.

"It's plain as day you want to ask me something, so why don't you just go ahead."

Miss Jane knew me too well. Maybe better than anyone, now that my grandparents were gone.

"All right." No sense beating around the bush. "What can you tell me about Miss Simone?"

"Do you mean her acting career?"

"I mean from her childhood, right on up until now."

I leaned back and watched as she furrowed her forehead in thought. She knew me well enough to know I wasn't being nosy.

"Hmm. I can't tell you a lot about her childhood. I believe her father died when she was small. Her mother was the housekeeper at Pennington House, and they lived in a cottage on Pennington property. She was a few years older than my friends and I. And by the time we were in our teens, she had left town." Something washed across her face, and I knew there was more. Something she was reluctant to mention.

"Was she involved with Forrest Pennington?"

Several shades of pink crossed her face. I waited.

Miss Jane cleared her throat. "That was the rumor. And yes, I guess it was true." She took a deep breath. "Yes, it was true."

Miss Jane wasn't usually all that reluctant to impart information, but I knew she'd been Miss Aggie's friend from the time they were small girls. I hated to press her.

I leaned toward her. "Can you tell me a little more?"

"All right. Don't badger me. I'm going to tell you."

Now that was the Miss Jane I knew. Relieved, I nodded. "Sorry."

"From what I've heard, Jenny Simon wasn't your typical bad girl. She simply fell hard for Forrest and set out to get him. Any way she could." She frowned and eyed me for a few seconds. "You need to keep in mind the things I'm telling you are what I've heard. I wasn't a witness to any of it."

"I understand. And I'll be sure to keep it in mind."

"According to the stories, Forrest returned Jenny's affection, and they were quite an item for a year or so, at least when he'd come home from wherever his job took him. Then Forrest left Cedar Chapel for New York City. Mrs. Pennington's family owned some sort of textile business, and they had offered him some posh position there."

A fit of coughing brought her to a halt.

I jumped up. "Let me get you some water. I'll be right back in a second." I hurried to the kitchen. Mabel had left everything shining and spotless. I took two bottles of water from the refrigerator and headed back to the great hall.

Miss Jane took the water gratefully and then leaned back.

"Where was I?" A brief frown appeared on her face, then she brightened.

"Oh yes, I remember. Forrest hadn't been in New York more than a couple of months before Jenny hightailed it out of here and followed him up there. I'm not sure how long they were together, but he never married her. Eventually, he left her for another woman. The one he did marry."

"So what became of Miss Simone?" I couldn't help but wonder how she got from her abandoned state to become a movie actress.

"Well, I'm not entirely sure what happened next. I believe she did some acting in New York City for a while, but somehow she ended up in Hollywood. It was quite a surprise to the people of Cedar Chapel to find their own Jenny Simon in movie magazines. She had become Jeannette Simone, and although she never actually became famous, she didn't do too badly." A look of admiration crossed Miss Jane's face, but she quickly concealed it.

"And that's her story, as far as I know."

She got up quickly, avoiding my eyes, and I had a pretty good idea she hadn't told me everything. But I had enough information to add fire to my suspicions that things weren't quite on the up-and-up with Miss Jeannette Simone.

"Thank you. I know it wasn't easy for you to divulge information that involved Miss Aggie's family."

Her eyes crinkled, and a warm smile appeared on her face. "Oh well, it's not like the information was a secret, and like I said, I'm not really sure how much of it is true."

She left the room, muttering something about playing

canasta. I continued to sit in the silent room, wondering how much of the information was true. It would be interesting to know what Miss Jane had decided to keep to herself. But I knew I'd better leave well enough alone for the time being.

The comforting squeak of the porch swing soothed me as I swung slowly back and forth with my eyes closed. I wished Benjamin would come over. I was supposed to be mad at him, but at the moment, I couldn't remember why. Oh yes. That's right. I got mad because he worried about me. How silly of me. I sighed. All I'd need to do is call, and he'd be here. I knew that. But I was too relaxed to get up and go to the phone. I really, really needed to get a cell phone. I'd been telling myself that for months.

"Hey, beautiful."

Benjamin. I smiled and opened my eyes. His smile sent shivers through me. And I felt like I was sinking into his deep blue eyes.

I knew I needed to apologize.

"I'm sorry about the things I said. I know you were worried about me, and I shouldn't have gotten so mad. I don't know what comes over me sometimes."

He smoothed my hair back from my forehead. Without thinking, I lifted my face, and he kissed my lips softly.

"I'm sorry, too, honey. I must have sounded really bossy. I'll try to tone it down and trust your judgment a little more."

He eased onto the swing beside me, curling his arm around my shoulders. It felt good to be cuddled a little tonight. I thought of the young Jenny Simon and her desperate need for a man who hadn't really loved her. How very, very tragic.

I snuggled closer to Benjamin. How could I have thought this wonderful, caring man might not be for me?

He kissed me on top of my head. "Sleepy, honey?"

"Umm-hmm." I yawned and sat up. "How was your day?"

He grinned. "Mrs. Riley's cat ran off again, and she's running an ad offering a reward for its return. Ten dollars, as usual."

I laughed. "Do you think she'll ever wise up? The same three boys take turns bringing Fluffy home and accepting the ten dollars every time the cat 'disappears.'"

"Personally, I think she does know. It's become a game to her, and she likes having someone to invite in for milk and cookies."

"Anything to top that?" The *Cedar Chapel Gazette* had some very entertaining submissions.

"Mrs. Alvin wrote a letter to the editor. She thinks the rosebushes on Tower Road and Chestnut need to be dug up. A bee flew into her open window as she was driving by."

"You're kidding." I swatted him on the arm.

"Nope. Scout's honor."

"Okay, anything serious?"

"Brad and Sharon Hill's little boy is in the hospital in Springfield again."

"Oh no." Seven-year-old Timmy had been diagnosed with leukemia when he was four. Many churches, including mine, had held round-the-clock prayer vigils. A year and a half ago he'd gone into remission, and the whole town had breathed a collective sigh of relief as well as prayers of thanksgiving. We'd held our breaths and prayed during that time that Timmy's remission would turn out to be a total healing.

"They aren't sure yet if it's the leukemia. They're doing tests." Grief twisted his face, and I reached over and placed my hand on his.

"We'll pray again. The whole town. Just like last time. Timmy is in God's hands. We just have to trust."

"I know. And I do." He squeezed my hand.

Benjamin had been a reporter for a newspaper in St. Louis for several years before he'd returned here and started up his family newspaper again. The tragic homicide and abuse cases he'd covered in the past had taken a toll on him. Even to the point where he'd lost his faith for a while. His love for God had prevailed, but sometimes, the memories came back.

We sat for a while without speaking. I was praying. And I was pretty sure Benjamin was, too.

"You haven't told me about your day yet." He lifted a strand of hair from behind my ear and began curling it around his finger.

I told him what Miss Jane had revealed about Jeannette Simone. And mentioned my suspicions.

He whistled. "Who would have thought it?"

"I know. Of course, we don't know how much is true."

"I could do some checking." Ben had sources I didn't even want to know about.

"Would you, Ben? I'd like to know if there's any basis in the rumors."

"Sure, I'll get on it right away."

"Thanks." I reached over and kissed his cheek.

"Don't you think it's strange how so many things lead

back to Pennington House and the Pennington family?"

"It is a little weird, but maybe it's just a coincidence."

"Maybe."

I yawned. Ben grinned and gave me a quick kiss.

"I'd better be going so you can get some sleep. I'll call you tomorrow." He waited until I was in the house then headed down the sidewalk and got into his truck.

I watched him pull away. My Benjamin. I almost floated upstairs.

———

I slept well and got up early. I really needed to tackle some cleaning chores today. Several of the ladies insisted on helping, and by midafternoon, the old lodge was beginning to shine.

"Miss Georgina, you haven't told me about the trip to Silver Dollar City." She was helping me dust the bookcases in the great hall.

"Oh, it was wonderful. Jane and I ate all day, and Eva scolded." She giggled. "We were very naughty."

"Oh well, you have to have some fun sometimes."

She nodded. "We sure had fun, all right."

"So, how were The Cajuns?"

Her eyes lit up. "I thought Cedric was going to tear the stage up. He and his accordion were on fire."

"It's been ages since I've been there. At least three or four years. Time just gets away from me these days." I sank into a brocade-covered chair. "I need a break."

"Of course you need a break. That's what we've been telling you." Her voice rose with excitement. "We're going back in October for the fall festival. You should come with us."

"Maybe I will. We'll take Benjamin along, too." My grandparents used to take Benjamin and me to the popular theme park often when we were kids. Those Silver Dollar City trips were about the only times the two of us had gotten along back then. There was something magical about the park that had drawn us together in spite of ourselves.

"Won't that be fun?" The sweet lady clapped her plump hands together.

"Yes," I said, catching her enthusiasm. "It's time I got out of my comfort zone. I might even ride the roller coaster." Yeah. Sure, I would. No one could drag me anywhere near that thing.

We finished up the dusting, and I went up to shower. While the hot streams of water massaged my shoulders, I let my mind wander to Miss Simone. She'd avoided me since I'd discovered her crying in the great room.

I wrapped myself in a plush terry robe and went to the table where I kept the notebook with my list. I jotted down some thoughts based on the information I'd received from Miss Jane.

Did Miss Simone hold anger against the Penningtons because of the way Forrest had treated her? Could she possibly be so bitter that she'd resort to murder? And what was Miss Jane holding back?

I reread the rest of my notes. I still had no answers. Only questions. Frustrated, I tossed the notebook back in the drawer and got dressed. Maybe I should give up on lists. Instead of getting clearer, everything seemed to be more confusing.

As I went downstairs, I heard the phone ring. Hoping it was Benjamin, I skipped down the last three steps and rushed into the kitchen.

Mabel handed me the phone. "It's for you. Some man."

Smiling, I took the phone. "Benjamin? Hi, handsome."

A deep, throaty chuckle from the earpiece revealed my mistake, and I caught my breath.

"Sorry, Miss Storm. I'm afraid I'm not Benjamin. But perhaps I should wish I were. Actually, this is Trent Stewart."

Say something, Victoria. I cleared my throat. "Hello, Mr. Stewart. Sorry about the mistake. I'm expecting a call from a friend."

"I would be honored to be your friend."

In spite of myself, I shivered. There was no denying I felt an attraction to this man.

I cleared my throat again. "May I help you in some way, Mr. Stewart?"

"Well, you could begin by dropping the Mr. Call me Trent. Please."

"Very well, Trent. What can I do for you?" I didn't want to sound rude, but I knew I couldn't give him any encouragement, either. I'd been guilty of that already.

"Actually, I'm calling to see if you've given any thought to my dinner invitation." An underlying hint of tension edged its way through his charming tone. Why would he be nervous or tense about a dinner date?

"Mr.—Trent, rather, I should have told you, I have a boyfriend. We're. . .well, actually I'm engaged. I'm sorry if I led you to believe I was available. I don't know what I was thinking."

"Ah, I see." He chuckled again. "Well, my dear, if you can forget that easily, perhaps there's hope for me yet. I'll see you soon, I'm sure. After all, I live here now."

"Yes, I'm sure I'll see you around. Cedar Chapel is a

small town. But Benjamin and I are definitely engaged. I didn't forget. I could never forget Benjamin. Good-bye."

But you did, Victoria. You know you did.

Shame washed over me. I loved Benjamin. So how could another man have this effect on me?

I breathed a prayer for strength and picked up the phone. I needed to hear Benjamin's voice.

He picked up on the second ring.

"Hi, sweetheart. I was just getting ready to call you."

"You were?" I laughed, sounding a little breathless even to myself. "I couldn't wait another minute."

"Umm-hmm. Words I love to hear. I'll be there before you know it." I felt a rush of love for him. And I knew. Whatever this thing was I felt for Trent, I'd nip it in the bud. It had nothing to do with my love for Benjamin Grant.

8

Sunday, after church, Phoebe stood in the foyer of the lodge next to Corky, her voice jumping with excitement. "I've been hearing Mom talk about her uncle, the adventurous Jack Riley, all my life. Somehow, I never truly thought he was real. He was more like a storybook character to me. And now, he's actually here!"

Corky grinned and shook his head. "I think she's star-struck."

"You two go on into the parlor while I get some lemonade. Ben is on his way over, so you can tell us both all about the amazing Uncle Jack."

When I entered the kitchen, the aroma of roast beef made my mouth water in anticipation. Mabel's cooking skills had turned out to be even better than she'd claimed.

She looked up from the cake she was frosting and gave me a nod.

"It smells wonderful in here, Mabel. I can't wait until dinner."

"Well, I don't know. The meat seemed a little stringy to me. I hope it'll be edible."

I grinned. After her interview, when she'd pretty much tooted her own horn about her cooking, she had continuously belittled every meal she'd cooked. And every one of them had been perfect.

"I'm sure it will be fine, as always. Is there plenty of lemonade? Corky and his girlfriend are here."

"Go ahead and take the pitcher. I'll make more. I just

hope this cake turns out all right. The batter seemed a little thick."

"I'm sure you have nothing to worry about, Mabel. It looks delicious."

When I walked into the parlor, Corky took the tray and placed it on the coffee table. He and Phoebe had claimed the love seat.

After I poured the lemonade, I sat on the sofa, facing the empty fireplace.

Benjamin arrived, and after greetings had been exchanged, he sat beside me.

"Phoebe's uncle is in town, and she was about to tell us about him."

"He's actually my great-uncle. He must be in his late eighties. But you'd never guess it. He's so sharp."

"So, tell us about him. He sounds intriguing." I smiled encouragingly.

Her blond curls bounced as she nodded.

"Okay. I don't know everything. I know he has an import/export business in Germany. I think he opened it in the late thirties. Mom remembers him as a dashing and handsome man, a world traveler. He stayed in Germany during the war and somehow managed to keep his business. My mother believes he may have helped rescue some Jewish people and smuggle them out of the country."

She continued to rave on and on about her wonderful Uncle Jack. Before she left, I invited her, her mother, her uncle, and Corky to dinner the following evening.

"Stay for dinner, Benjamin?" I asked, after Corky and Phoebe had left.

"You twisted my arm." He grinned, and we went out

to sit on the porch swing until dinner was ready.

"I've started researching Jeannette Simone. So far, I've only come up with well-known information about her career and a few pictures of her house in Beverly Hills. Does she still own it, by the way?"

I nodded. "She told me when she reserved the suite she has a home there." I sighed. "You'll keep searching, won't you?"

"Absolutely." He tipped my chin up. "If there's anything to be found, I'll find it for you."

"Maybe it's all my imagination. I have these suspicions running through my head and very few facts to base them on."

"The sheriff doesn't seem to be doing much better. He says he has no real leads."

"I think he knows more than he's telling. The last time I talked to him, I felt he was hiding something from me." I shook my head. "But that could be my imagination as well."

"Victoria, don't worry so much. Somehow, we'll get to the truth of the matter. Either through our own investigation or the sheriff's."

"I hope you're right."

Frank and Martin came out on the porch and started talking about football. My cue to leave and go help with dinner preparations.

The roast was wonderful, as I knew it would be. The chocolate turtle cake was magnificent, which was no surprise, either.

The seniors were excited that Jack Riley was coming to dinner the next day. Few of them actually remembered him, but apparently, he'd been rather a legend in the town.

Suddenly, the sound of silver against crystal interrupted the chatter, and everyone grew quiet.

Frank stood, tapping his water glass with his spoon, with an enormous grin on his face.

When he had everyone's attention, he took a deep breath.

"Folks, I have an announcement to make. Well. . .that is"—he looked down at Miss Evalina, and the tenderness on his face spoke volumes—"Eva and I have an announcement to make."

I held my breath. This was it. Finally. The moment I'd expected six months ago.

"Eva has done me the great and undeserved honor of agreeing to become my wife." He sat down next to the blushing bride-to-be and took her hand.

After a moment of shocked silence from everyone but me, applause broke out, followed by exclamations of congratulations.

"How long have you two been planning this?" Miss Jane shrilled with excitement.

"Well, we've been discussing it for a couple of months. But she wouldn't give me a definite yes until last week."

"Why, Eva. You've been so mum. I can't believe you kept such a happy secret from us." Miss Simone smiled, which she hadn't done much of lately. She seemed truly happy for the engaged couple.

Miss Georgina rushed over and gave Miss Evalina a hug, followed by Miss Jane. The two fluttered around Miss Evalina like teenagers.

"Congratulations, Frank." Benjamin held his hand out to the man who'd taken him in when he was a young boy. "You're a lucky man, you know."

"I do know." Frank gave Miss Evalina's hand another squeeze, and she smiled into his eyes.

I waited until things calmed down a little, then I stood. "Frank, Miss Evalina. I can't say how thrilled I am for you both. I pray you'll have many years of happiness." *Please, God, let it be so.*

"Well, I'll be." Apparently, Martin had just found his voice. "Congratulations, Frank, Eva."

"So when's the wedding day?" Miss Jane asked. Her face glowed as she looked at her lifelong friends.

"We haven't set a date yet." Miss Evalina spoke softly and smiled at Frank. "We'll let you know just as soon as we do."

The glow in Miss Evalina's eyes was proof enough that all her uncertainty and doubts were gone.

Once more, Benjamin and I sat on the porch swing, enjoying the late August evening. Tomorrow was the first of September, and nights in this area of the Ozarks were cooling a little.

The door opened, and Miss Simone stepped out onto the porch.

"May I join you?"

Surprised, I moved over closer to Benjamin and made room on the swing. "Of course you can. I'll enjoy the company."

"Wait, Miss Simone." Benjamin stood and got a cushioned wicker rocker from the other side of the porch. "Here, this will be more comfortable than the wooden slats."

"Thank you, Mr. Grant." She eased herself down onto the seat, groaning a little. Ben sat beside me.

"Please call me Benjamin, Miss Simone."

Miss Simone inclined her head slightly.

I wondered what she was up to. She'd never really sought me out for conversation before. *I really have to stop this. Maybe she just wants to sit out on the porch.*

"It's really nice out tonight, isn't it?" She glanced out over the lawn, which, thanks to Martin and Frank's care, had remained green and lush even during July and August.

"Yes," I said. "I love it out here this time of night. It's so quiet and peaceful."

"Yes." She picked at the fabric of her slacks and cleared her throat.

Okay, maybe she *was* up to something. I decided to fish a little. "So how do you like being back in your hometown, now that you've settled in?"

"Oh, it's fine. Things are a lot different nowadays. And all my family is gone. But it's nice to be back anyway."

"I know it's a lot different from the life you've been used to."

"Well, actually, for the past ten years or so, I've lived rather quietly, not getting out much."

Since she was eighty-five, I would think so, but I kept that little thought to myself, not wishing to offend her.

"I watched one of your movies a couple of months ago. I think it was called *The Girl on the Midnight Train*."

She laughed. "Goodness, where did you find that antique? That was filmed in 1947." A rather dreamy look crossed her face. "Tom Carpenter and Ann Sheldon starred in that one. I was the supporting actress."

"I enjoyed it. You were very good." And I meant it.

"Yes, well, thank you. That was a long time ago. I haven't acted since 1955." Pity rose up in me at the wistful look that crossed her face. It must be hard to be an ex-diva. But at least she'd had her day. I wondered what her life had been like during those years.

She sat up straight and composed her face. "But that's enough about me. Have you heard anything from Aggie? Is she coming home soon?"

Now what in the world brought that on? I wasn't aware of any special rapport between the two ladies.

"I really don't know. I suppose when it suits her or when they solve the murder." I looked to see if she'd react. Was that a shadow that appeared in her eyes? Or just interest?

"Yes, I wonder if Sheriff Turner has any evidence yet." A slight tremor shook her voice. Was she nervous about something?

"If he has, he isn't sharing it. But then, why would he?" I paused, then added, "I think he probably knows more than he's telling."

"How about you, Benjamin? You're a newspaperman. Has the sheriff said anything to you?"

Benjamin laughed. "I'm probably the last person he'd confide in, if he has information he's not wanting out."

She caught her breath then stood up. "You could be right. Well, I'm very tired. I think I'll retire for the night."

"Good night, Miss Simone. Sleep well."

"Thank you. Good night."

I looked over at Benjamin. "Well, don't you think that was strange?"

"Maybe she was simply curious. But it was a little strange for her to get so talkative all of a sudden. She's hardly said a word to me before."

"And she doesn't talk to me very much, either." I frowned and tapped my nails against the wooden slats. "I think she came outside to find out if we knew anything. But why?"

Benjamin shook his head. "C'mon, Vickie. You don't really think a little old lady went to Pennington House in the middle of the night, followed an old man into a dark tunnel, picked up a heavy rock, and conked him on the head, do you?"

Exasperated, I glared at him. But he was right. It was a preposterous idea. Still. . .

"But why would she come back to Cedar Chapel when all her friends and family are gone? She has the house in Beverly Hills, and she must know people there."

"Maybe. But honey, even if she's bitter because of the way Forrest Pennington treated her, don't you think it's a little farfetched that she'd wait all this time then come here and kill someone on Pennington property to get even?"

"What if there's something other than revenge motivating her?"

"Okay, that's possible. But I still can't see her being involved in a murder."

"But you will continue to investigate her, won't you?"

"Of course. I promised I would. I just don't think I'm going to find anything."

I sighed. "I wish this was over. Miss Georgina is still nervous every time she leaves the lodge."

"I know the ladies are nervous, honey. And to be honest, I'll be glad when it's behind us too. I don't like having to worry about you. Please be careful." He reached over and tucked a strand of hair behind my ear.

I laid my head on his shoulder. "I'll be careful. I promise."

"That's all I ask." He leaned over and kissed me softly. "I'll call you tomorrow, okay?"

"All right. Good night."

I sat for a while after he left. Why couldn't I leave this whole matter to Sheriff Turner? I sat up. Maybe I should tell him what I knew about Miss Simone. Immediately, I tossed the idea away. He'd laugh his head off.

I yawned. I needed to get some rest. Mabel was off tomorrow, and I would need to help Miss Jane prepare for the guests.

I went to my room and got into my pajamas. But by now, I was wide awake. I sat in my recliner and picked up a book. This one was a romance about a modern-day cowboy and a lady vet. I'd laid off suspense for a while. There was more than enough suspense going on in my life right now.

The book was very entertaining and kept my attention for a while, until an elderly lady came on the scene. Then, Miss Simone popped back into my mind. With a sigh, I laid down the book and picked up my notebook and pen.

What if it was true that Miss Simone had a motive other than revenge?

Who did she talk to on the phone that upset her so? Could there be an accomplice?

Why was she suddenly so interested in the

progress of the murder investigation?

I paused in my writing. Maybe I should ask her outright. But then, if she was guilty, she'd be warned that I was on to her.

I looked over the list, and my eyes rested on Clyde Foster's name. Could Clyde and Miss Simone be in it together? I had no idea if they knew each other, but it was possible, wasn't it?

And what did Miss Jane know that she wasn't mentioning?

I groaned. My mind was whirling, and I was getting nowhere. I crawled into bed and picked my Bible up from the nightstand. Only God could settle my thoughts. And just maybe, then, I'd think of something new. Something I was missing.

9

Jack Riley, at eighty-six, had undeniable flare and charm. Mabel, either out of compassion for Miss Jane and me or for curiosity, came in and helped prepare and serve dinner. She was clearly smitten as our guest continued to praise everything she placed in front of him. And even Miss Jane and Miss Georgina seemed mesmerized as he kept the conversation going throughout dinner.

Miss Simone, pleading illness, asked for a tray, which I took to her room before we went in to dine. She didn't appear ill to me, but I knew older people often had aches and pains not visible to others.

Phoebe's mother hadn't come, due to a prior obligation, but Phoebe gazed adoringly at her great-uncle. I was happy to notice he singled her out for attention from time to time.

I decided, in honor of such a distinguished guest, to retire to the great hall instead of the parlor after dinner. I'd laid a fire for ambience, figuring the size of the room would prevent it from becoming too warm.

We sat on sofas and chairs arranged comfortably near the fireplace.

"Mr. Riley, Phoebe told me you own an import/export business in Germany and have traveled extensively." I leaned forward in my chair and smiled. "I must admit I'm intrigued. Would you mind telling us about some of your adventures?"

He chuckled and stroked the white goatee that adorned his chin. "I believe my niece may see me as much more of an adventurer than I am. But it is true I've done a great deal of traveling. I'd be more than happy to tell you some of the events of those travels."

"Tell them about the emperor, Uncle Jack." Phoebe's eyes gleamed with pride in her elderly relative.

He shook his finger at her, but his smile softened the action. "Ah yes, my dear. You wish to hear about the emperor. You must remember, this was many years ago. It was a very small eastern country which I believe is now in the process of converting to a democratic government." He took a sip from his teacup and then set it down.

"I heard about a certain diamond that was housed in the palace. A wealthy client's wife craved it, and they'd given me almost unlimited funds to obtain it. My party and I arrived there by camel train and were warmly welcomed.

"The emperor insisted on having a banquet in my honor. I think he planned to haggle over the diamond, for which he obviously held no sentimental value. During this lavish banquet, the palace was attacked. I won't go into details, but I was able to protect the emperor until his guards could apprehend the attackers."

"Uncle Jack! You're being modest." Phoebe interrupted. "You saved his life."

"Well, I suppose I did, at that." He reached over and patted her hand. "At any rate, the emperor was extremely grateful and insisted on giving me the diamond. And that is the end of the story."

Throughout the rest of the evening, upon our insistence, he regaled us with tales of his travels. I could understand why Phoebe was so enthralled.

Just as he seemed to reach the end of his stories, or

at least the end of his willingness to tell them, Phoebe spoke up. "You haven't told us about the Jewish people you helped during World War II. Please do."

Hesitation crossed his countenance, and for the first time, his eyes spoke reluctance. Interesting, I thought.

I stood. "Let me get some more tea. Phoebe, would you like to help?"

"Yes, of course." She jumped up and followed as I pushed the tea cart into the kitchen.

"Isn't he wonderful, Victoria?" Phoebe's blue eyes shone as she filled the creamer and put a small bowl of lemon slices on the tray.

"Yes, he is absolutely wonderful. But I believe he's getting tired. Maybe he'd rather wait for another time to tell us any more."

"Maybe. If he doesn't want to, I won't insist."

I grinned. How good of her, I thought. Ah. There I went with the sarcasm again. At least this time, I kept it to myself.

We were welcomed enthusiastically when we returned with the tea cart. Benjamin, Corky, and Mr. Riley stood at the front window, laughing. Martin and Frank stood next to them, grinning. I wondered what they'd been talking about. The men returned to their seats, and I poured tea for those who wanted it.

Mr. Riley sat silently for a moment, and I assumed he had either forgotten Phoebe's request or had decided against it.

He took a deep drink of the hot brew and glanced at Phoebe. "So you are curious about the Jewish situation."

My skin crawled at the term "Jewish situation." Wasn't that what the Nazis had called their desire to get rid of an entire race of people?

Be fair, Victoria. It's just words. He didn't mean it like you heard it.

Apparently, I was the only one who had picked up on the connection. Everyone turned to him in anticipation.

"Yes, Uncle. If you're sure you don't mind." She smiled at me, and I smiled back.

He sat for a moment, obviously deep in thought. It seemed as though he had left us. As though he'd returned to another place, another time. His face appeared haunted. I shivered.

"It was a terrible time." He cleared his throat. "I haven't spoken of it in many years, and I hardly know where to begin.

"When Hitler came into power, he seemed a hero. His charismatic personality won nearly everyone over to his ideas. And in the beginning, the ideas he put forth sounded wonderful. Ideas for a new Germany. A land of peace and prosperity. Of course, I was an American, and my business at that time was pretty much in the hands of my managers while I traveled. Once the war broke out, I returned to Berlin to try to protect my business. America was not involved yet, so I hoped my company would not be affected. I was horrified to discover that the rumors I'd been hearing were true. Jewish citizens were being spat upon, forbidden any rights whatsoever, including education. One day, I saw a guard slap a teenage girl and scream at her simply for sitting on a public bench."

He paused and ran his hand over his face, as though attempting to wipe away the image.

"Mr. Riley, if this is too difficult for you, please don't continue," I said. I reached over on impulse and laid my hand on his arm.

He patted my hand and smiled. "No, no, I'll be all right. It was over a long time ago." He picked up a glass of water and took a deep drink.

"I knew something terrible was coming. It was obvious to anyone who didn't have their eyes covered. My Jewish acquaintances were suddenly frightened. Most wanted to leave the country. Of course, by then, the only way they could leave was to desert their homes and businesses. They weren't allowed to take anything with them.

"I began to hear of entire families disappearing overnight. Some had managed to get away, but most were unaccounted for.

"I had some connections throughout Europe and the United States. But visas were becoming more and more difficult to obtain. There were organizations from Israel who had come to Germany to help evacuate people. In the beginning, they helped families, but after a while, they could take only children."

As he spoke, my mind took me to a dark place and I felt as though I were suffocating.

"I did what I could to help. I managed to get some of their belongings, mostly jewels and artwork, out of the country and into France and other sympathetic countries, so they could claim them later. But of course, as the Nazis conquered more and more of the European nations, our efforts were mostly in vain. At least we were able to rescue some of the people." Once more, he wiped his hand over his face and then took a deep breath. "There really isn't much more to say about it. We saved very few compared to the many who lost their lives."

"What happened to your business, and what did you do?"

Not now, Martin. Can't you see how hard this is for him?

But Martin continued. "Surely, you didn't stay, once the United States entered the war."

"No, I left my company in the hands of two managers and spent the next few years in England and the United States. I hadn't much hope of a business to go back to, especially since I was American. But after the war, I found to my surprise and delight that the company was still operating. I still have no idea how my managers were able to keep it running. I was in the red, but the war was over, and many of my American clients were ready to buy again. I spent the next few years traveling and getting my business built back up, and before too long, Riley Imports/ Exports was doing well."

"And it's still doing well," Phoebe stated, beaming at her uncle.

"Yes, very well. Now, however, it is in the capable hands of my daughter." A troubled look appeared momentarily in his eyes, but he immediately smiled. "And that, my dear, is the story of your old uncle's life."

Something bothered me. Something he'd said. But what? I couldn't put my finger on it. But something was definitely wrong.

By the time Phoebe and her uncle left, the seniors were ready to retire for the night. Benjamin and I returned to our favorite spot. The porch swing. It had been there for as long as I could remember. The chains had been replaced, and I remember Grandpa replaced slats over the years, but it still felt and looked the same as it always had. Benjamin and I had fought and made up time and again on that swing. I remembered when we were younger. A mumbled, embarrassed apology, usually from Ben, after he'd tormented me in one way or another. And for some reason, although I'd claimed to despise him, I'd always accepted his apology. It always felt so good afterward. It still did.

I chuckled.

"What's so funny?" Benjamin grabbed my hand as we pushed the swing back and forth.

"I was just remembering you rubbing your foot right there on the porch and saying, 'Sorry.'"

"I still do that, don't I?"

"Well, pretty much, but now when you say 'I'm sorry,' you don't look like you'd rather chew nails than apologize."

He threw his head back and laughed. "Was I that bad?"

"Absolutely."

He cupped his hand under my chin and looked into my eyes. "I'm glad you always said you forgave me. It's nice to have those memories."

I leaned back and closed my eyes. The backfiring of a car jerked me out of my reverie.

"Wow, that almost sounded like a gunshot."

"No, it didn't."

"It did to me."

Ben laughed and squeezed my hand.

"What do you think of Jack Riley?" I asked.

"Oh, he seems like a nice old guy. Had quite a life, it seems." He glanced at me. "Why? What do you think of him?" Was that a guarded look on Ben's face?

"Oh, I just wondered. What did you think of his story?"

He groaned and straightened up on the swing. Now I knew his guarded look had nothing to do with Jack Riley and everything to do with me. "Victoria, what are you getting at?"

"Nothing. I'm not getting at anything. It's just. . . something about his story bothered me." I bit my lip, waiting for him to object.

"What about his story bothered you?" Benjamin didn't have to sound so pained, did he?

"I don't know. Something. I can't remember. It'll come to me, though."

He pushed up from the swing and gave me an exasperated look. "You know what, Vickie? You have the most suspicious mind of anyone I've ever known."

"I know." And I did know. "I'm sorry. It's probably nothing."

"I think you need to get away. Forget this whole thing for a while. Pretty soon, you'll be suspecting me."

"Don't be silly. I'd never suspect you. And I didn't say I suspected Mr. Riley of anything. I just said something bothered me."

He scowled. I'd done it again. Maybe it was time to change the subject.

"But since you mentioned getting away, Miss Georgina invited us to go with them to Silver Dollar City when they go back. What do you think?"

"Sounds great. I haven't been there in years."

"Me, either. We should go. She said they'll probably go in October."

"Okay, count me in."

"Remember the time at Silver Dollar City when you were supposed to be watching me while Grandma and

Grandpa bought some baskets or something? I think you were ten and I was eight. And you ran off to watch some guy doing rope tricks?"

"Yeah, I remember how scared I was when I realized you hadn't followed me. Believe me, when I apologized that time, I meant it. With all my heart."

"I know. I was a pretty wise chick, even when I was eight."

He grinned. "I'd better go. We both need to get to sleep." He stretched then leaned over and kissed me. "Good night, honey."

"Good night." I watched him walk to his truck. He waved as he drove away. I was relieved that I'd averted tension, or at least an argument, between us. But why couldn't I have kept my mouth shut in the first place?

I cleaned the tea things and loaded the dishwasher then went up to my room.

As I passed Miss Simone's suite, I thought I heard a noise. I stopped at her door and listened. She was crying. I tapped lightly.

A moment later, she opened her door slightly. Her eyes were red. "Yes? What is it?"

"Are you all right? I thought I heard you crying."

She took a sobbing breath before she spoke. "Yes, I'm fine. I'm watching a sad movie."

"Oh. I'm so sorry to have disturbed you."

"That's quite all right." She closed the door.

I walked to my room. I hadn't heard her television, and the room had been dark. Now why would she lie to me?

She could have simply told me to mind my own business. It wouldn't be the first time. I shrugged and climbed the steep stairs to the third floor.

By the time I'd gotten ready for bed, I still hadn't managed to shrug off the incident. Something was going on with Miss Simone. And even if it had nothing to do with the murder, I needed to find out what was distressing her so.

I took a bottle of water from the small refrigerator I kept in my room. Grabbing my book, I climbed into bed, sitting against my propped-up pillows. I shifted around, trying to get comfortable. Grandma used to have a bed cushion with arms that was perfect for reading. I wondered where it was. Maybe in her old sewing room. I'd look for it tomorrow.

I opened my book and was soon lost in the story of the cowboy and the lady vet. I was halfway through the book when I felt myself nodding off. Yawning, I put my book away and readjusted my pillows. Once more, I began to drift, when suddenly I sat up, wide awake. It had suddenly hit me what bothered me about Jack Riley's story.

He said he'd had buyers in the states after the war. What did they buy? There was practically nothing left after the war. The Nazis had stolen most of the valuables, secreting them away. Years passed before things started turning up again, and some never did.

He said he had helped to send valuables out of the country for Jewish people. Had he actually stashed them away somewhere and those were the items he sold after the war? Was the story of how he had helped the Jews a cover-up for the fact he was stealing from them?

He'd seemed so broken up when he talked about the

mistreatment of the Jews in Germany. That could have been an act. Or maybe not. Maybe in his older years, he was suffering from the memories of what he had done.

Victoria, stop it! I lay back on my pillows, and my eyes filled with tears. Tears I couldn't hold back. Now I was seeing Phoebe's uncle as a monster. What did I know about the import/export business? Nothing. That's what. I seemed to be seeing evil in everyone I came in contact with.

Lord, please help me to think clearly and not go off on ridiculous tangents. I'd done this all my life, but lately, I seemed to be getting worse. *And Father, please help me to be led by Your Spirit and leave the results in Your hands instead of making impulsive judgments about everyone.*

10

"Okay, Buster," I yelled. "I'll be there in a minute."

I had a throbbing headache from lack of sleep due to my worrying about, first, Miss Simone, and then Jack Riley. And Buster's barking, which continued to reverberate throughout the house, wasn't helping. He had the deepest, loudest bark of any dog I'd ever known.

"I'll finish putting these pots away," Mabel said, tossing me a compassionate glance. "If you don't take him out, none of us will have any peace."

I hung the dish towel on its rack and shook my head in apology. "Sorry. I'll help when I get back."

"No need. I'm about done cleaning up in here. How many for lunch?"

"Just Miss Simone and me, I guess. Everyone else is at the center. Maybe just a chicken salad and some fruit."

Buster stopped barking and wagged his tail as he saw me walk into the hallway. He nudged the leash that hung on a hook by the door. When I stepped toward him, the tail wagged faster and his mouth opened in what I always insisted was a smile.

"Ready to go out, boy?" He jumped around with excitement as I grabbed the leash and snapped it onto his collar. Once I opened the door, he practically dragged me through it.

"Slow down, Buster. Who's leading who?"

Ignoring me, he galloped down the sidewalk, dragging me behind him. I'd been threatening to enroll him in obedience training for months. The time had come to look into that.

"Hi, Buster!" The ten-year-old boy across the street whistled, and Buster turned and rushed in his direction. The ornery kid laughed and ran around the corner of his house, with Buster in pursuit and me running and stumbling behind.

By the time I'd managed to yank him to a stop, we were behind the house and the boy was nowhere in sight. Buster looked up at me and whined.

"It's okay, boy. You're not the one he's tormenting. It's me." Bobby Hansen and all his siblings lived to make my life miserable. I knew they'd been out to get me ever since I made the mistake of engaging in a snowball fight with them last winter. They'd pelted me good, but I'd won by escaping in my car after throwing one well-aimed snowball. Maybe I should apologize.

Buster settled down after a while and was content to stroll along at my pace. We'd walked several blocks when I remembered I needed computer paper, so I turned toward the square. I'd get a small package at the drugstore. Just enough to keep me going until I could get over to the office supply store in Branson.

I hooked Buster's leash to a post in front of the store, hoping there were no cats in the vicinity, and went inside.

The owner, Mr. Taylor, sat on a stool behind the counter, reading the *Gazette*. He looked up as I approached.

"Hello, Victoria. What can I get for you?"

"Just computer paper today. I'll get it."

I made my choice and headed for the cash register. "Anything interesting in the *Gazette* today?"

"Timmy's out of the hospital." He rang up the sale and counted out my change. "It wasn't the leukemia this time. Just some new strain of flu."

"Oh, that's wonderful! What a relief." The whole town had been on pins and needles waiting to find out.

"Yes, they've started a fund at the bank to help Brad and Sharon pay the hospital bill."

"That's great. I'll head over there before I go home."

I unhooked Buster from the post, and he immediately tried to head back home.

"Not yet, Buster. One more stop." I walked to the bank and secured his leash to another post.

Phoebe waved as I walked in and smiled as I stepped over to her window.

"What did you think of Uncle Jack?" She entered some data into the computer on the counter and then looked up.

"He's very charming, Phoebe. He seems to have lived quite a life." There. Nothing in either of those statements to reveal my suspicion.

"I'd like to make a donation to Timmy's hospital fund. Can you take care of it?"

"Mrs. Stanton is handling that." She motioned to an office on my right.

"Thanks."

After I'd made the donation, Phoebe and I chatted a few minutes and I left. Buster and I headed back to the lodge. The aroma of coffee and pastry wafted across the air as I walked past the Mocha Java. Pausing a moment, I considered going in but resisted the temptation, not wanting to tie Buster up again.

I was a half block away from home when I saw Mrs. Miller in her front yard. Before I could turn and go another way, she saw me and waved. Groaning, I waved

102 Miss Aggie Cries Murder

back. Grandma had always told me Janis Miller had a voracious curiosity, a loose tongue, and a heart of gold. I knew my grandmother was right.

She grinned and waved her pruning shears as I stopped in front of her.

"It's a nice day for a walk, isn't it, dear?"

"Yes, ma'am. Wonderful. Buster and I both enjoyed it."

"I wish I'd seen you leave." She scrunched her forehead, and deep lines appeared. "I'd have gone with you."

"I'm sorry. Maybe next time." Thinking of Grandma made me sentimental, and I added, "I'll be walking him again later, if you want to go along."

Her face brightened. "Why, thank you, dear. But I'm having guests for dinner, so I'll be busy."

"Oh, that's all right. We'll do it another time," I said, trying not to look relieved. "I'd better get on home."

"Who was that gentleman who came with Phoebe and Corky last night?" The innocent look on her face didn't gel. I knew her too well.

"Phoebe's great-uncle, Jack Riley. He used to live here when he was a boy."

"Oh, it must have been before I married Gerald and moved here. I'm from Lebanon, you know. Have you ever been there?"

"A few times. Just passing through." Lebanon was between Springfield and Fort Leonard Wood. I still remembered stopping at a little downtown café there with my grandparents, on the way to our camping site.

"I'll ask Gerald if he remembers Mr. Riley." She brushed her hand on her apron and peered at me. "I've remembered something else about Jenny Simon you might want to know."

That got my attention. "Oh?" I tried not to sound too eager.

"Yes," she said, nodding. "Now, you need to realize this is a rumor. I have no idea if it's true or not. But I thought you should know, with her living in your house. Your grandmother's house, at that."

"I'll remember it may not be true." *Just, please, get on with it.*

"Well, all right. I hope I'm not spreading gossip."

"I know you'd never gossip, Mrs. Miller." I almost laughed.

"Hmm. You're not being sarcastic, are you?"

"No, ma'am. You know Grandma taught me better than that." Which was true. Unfortunately, it was one lesson that didn't take.

I knew she was about to talk herself out of telling me, so I figured I'd better use some strategy.

"It's okay, Mrs. Miller. I wouldn't want you to go against your conscience."

"Well, I think I'd better tell you. I'll just say it right out. You see, there was talk of a baby."

"A baby? Who had a baby?"

She gave me an exasperated look. "Now who are we talking about? Jenny Simon."

I laughed. "Well, that's not so shocking, is it? She probably married sooner or later."

"No, dear. The baby, if there really was one, was born a few months after her affair with Forrest Pennington ended."

I caught my breath. Could this be the clue I'd been searching for?

"When did you hear this rumor? And who told you?"

"I think I overheard it at some luncheon or other. Many years ago, of course. I'd gone to the ladies' room to powder my nose. I believe it was Aggie and Jane who were talking about it." She nodded. "Yes, I'm sure it was. Maybe you could ask them. Only don't tell them where you heard it."

"I won't. Thank you for telling me." I yanked Buster away from the flowering bush he was sniffing and said good-bye.

Could this rumor be true? And if so, was it significant to the murder? Or was it simply another incident of young Aggie Pennington trying to cause trouble for someone? Like she did with Miss Evalina. No matter. It was the closest thing to a clue I'd come across so far.

Not wanting to be overheard, I went to my room to call Benjamin.

He answered on the first ring. "Hi, honey. I was just about to come over. I've turned up something about Miss Simone. It may or may not mean anything."

"Good, I have something to tell you about her, too. But I don't think we'd better talk here."

"How about lunch? I was planning to ask you anyway. We could go to the steakhouse in Caffee Springs."

"Sounds good. I'll be ready."

I changed into a denim skirt and plaid cotton blouse and ran a comb through my unruly curls. A touch of lipstick and I was ready.

I ducked into the kitchen. "Mabel, I'm going to Caffee Springs with Benjamin, so it'll just be you and Miss

Simone for lunch. Do you have everything you need for dinner?"

"Sure do. Go along and have fun."

The drive to Caffee Springs always relaxed me. Even when someone else was driving. Oak trees and wildflowers lined the two-lane highway. The leaves would be starting to turn in another month, and I waited eagerly for fall, my favorite season. But for now, I basked in the gorgeous colors of summer.

"You sure look pretty in that cute little skirt." Benjamin grinned and squeezed my hand.

"Thank you very much," I said, returning the grin. "But please get that hand back on the steering wheel where it belongs."

He chuckled but put both hands on the wheel. He knew the hills and curves still made me nervous. I didn't know if I'd ever get used to them, even though I'd spent my summers and most of my holidays here with my grandparents. I knew it was silly, when I was accustomed to Dallas traffic.

We pulled into Caffee Springs, a pretty little tourist town, which wasn't nearly as old as the chamber of commerce tried to convey. But the ancient look of some of the buildings seemed to fool the tourists.

The smoky aroma of the steakhouse made me realize I'd only had toast and orange juice for breakfast. The hostess led us to a rustic booth and left menus, promising glasses of water, which promptly arrived.

The food was good, and the server knew her stuff. I felt myself relax even more.

After our meal, we accepted iced-tea refills but refused dessert.

I put my elbows on the table and leaned forward.

"Okay, tell me what you've found."

Benjamin smiled a quirky little smile. "I'm impressed that you've waited this long to mention it. I wasn't sure I'd get to eat my lunch."

I nodded. "All right. I know I can be overly eager at times. But I've exercised self-control long enough, so stop teasing and tell me. Okay?"

He nodded and reached into his back pocket.

The folded newspaper was yellow with age, and somehow, I knew it was important.

He unfolded it and held it out to me. "This is a 1940 version of a Hollywood tabloid. So it may not be true."

The article claimed that Hollywood starlet, Jeannette Simone, had a child conceived out of wedlock. It admitted there was no proof about the father but mentioned several actors who had been seen around town with the "provocative" Jeannette.

"Oh, Ben. This is the same news I have. Mrs. Miller told me today there had been a rumor about a child. Apparently, it's true."

"So I guess I'll keep digging and see if I can find anything else about it."

"Mrs. Miller seemed to think Miss Aggie and Miss Jane might know something. I'm going to talk to Miss Jane tonight, if I can get her away from the others."

"Are you sure it's that important? I mean, a baby out of wedlock isn't exactly a motive for murder."

"I know, but things were different in the forties, you know. Benjamin, do you think Forrest Pennington was the father?"

"Honey, we're just guessing at this point. I have no idea. Remember, we're not really sure there was a baby. This could all be gossip."

"Yes, but something like this. Surely there's some truth to it."

We were both quiet on the drive back to Cedar Chapel. Benjamin dropped me off at the lodge then drove on to the *Gazette* office.

I waited eagerly for the seniors to get back from the center. Finally, they trooped in. Before I could get Miss Jane aside, she went into the rec room with Miss Georgina and was soon deep into a game of canasta. I didn't want to interrupt them, so I decided to wait until later to talk to her.

Frustrated, I went to Grandma's sewing room on the third floor and started boxing up rolls of fabric. I'd been putting it off long enough. If I was going to have an apartment on the third floor, it had to be done. I ran my hand over a partial bolt of blue silk. It was the material Grandma had made my costume from the year I'd played Mary in the church Christmas program.

"I wish you were here, Grandma," I whispered. "I'm so confused. What would you tell me to do if you were here? Just drop it all? Maybe you'd tell me I've been reading too many mystery books. Like you used to." Memories flooded me. Memories of the young Victoria Storm, "casing the joint" in search of the "crook" who'd stolen Grandma's thimble. I felt my lips tilt in a smile at the memory of Grandma laughing and calling me Nancy Drew.

Was my present situation a childish game as well?

I remembered Miss Aggie's fear as we sat in the parlor the night the body was found. And how her fear had driven her away. This was no game. Whoever the dead man was, the crime had happened at Pennington House. A house full of mysteries. Miss Aggie didn't think it was a coincidence that Pennington House was chosen as the place to commit the crime. And I felt strongly she was right.

I packed away the rest of the fabric and went down to dinner.

Miss Simone sat across from me. She seemed so prim and proper. But I'd seen an emotional side to her. And who was to say what she was like when she was young? If it were true that she'd had an affair with Forrest Pennington, and it seemed that it was, why couldn't there have been a child from the relationship?

Miss Simone stayed downstairs after dinner and joined Miss Jane and Miss Georgina in a game of Yahtzee. It didn't seem likely I'd get to have a private conversation with Miss Jane tonight.

I walked into the foyer just in time to see Miss Evalina going upstairs. I wondered if she knew anything about the baby. I knew she didn't indulge in gossip, so anything I learned from her would more than likely be accurate.

I went upstairs and tapped on her door.

"Come in, Victoria." Now how did she know who it was?

I opened the door and went into Miss Evalina's room, one of my favorite places in the lodge. Welcoming warmth greeted me, and I breathed in the familiar, subtle aroma of lavender.

"How did you know it was me?"

She smiled. "I saw you watching from the foyer when I reached the landing. Come sit down. Tell me what's on your mind."

I went to the sofa and sank into the soft brocade-covered cushions beside Miss Evalina.

Being with her was the next best thing to being with my grandmother. I explained what I wanted to know.

11

"Victoria, why do you care about a sixty-year-old rumor?" Miss Evalina stared at me in disapproval.

"Please don't look at me like that. I promise I'm not asking out of curiosity." I could bear almost anyone's disapproval but hers.

"Then please explain yourself. I'll need a valid reason if I'm to discuss the matter."

"Miss Simone has been behaving strangely lately." I told her about the mysterious phone calls and of finding the lady in tears.

"I'm not sure I understand what you're getting at."

"The phone calls sounded like someone was threatening her. At the very least, something frightened her. And I started wondering why she would come back to Cedar Chapel after all these years. Considering how wealthy she is, why would she move into the lodge? It's not as though she had been close friends with all of you, as the case was with Miss Aggie. She doesn't even seem to like it here, and to be honest, I don't think she likes any of us, either. Then, the murder happening soon after, and finding out about her relationship with Aggie's brother and his abandonment of her. . ."

"All right, I follow your line of thought. But it doesn't make sense to think she came here and murdered someone just because she had a bad relationship sixty years ago."

"Okay, that bothered me, too. But what if there *is* a child, and she feels he deserves a share in the Pennington inheritance?"

Miss Evalina frowned, and a thoughtful look appeared in her eyes. "I don't know. It seems rather far-fetched, doesn't it? And why wait so long? The child, if there is one, would be in his sixties."

I sighed. When she put it that way, it did sound rather ridiculous.

"Maybe there was another reason. I don't know. But it's the only lead I have."

She reached over and patted my hand. "Child, why must you try to solve the problems of the world?"

"Not the world, Miss Evalina, just our world. Miss Aggie shouldn't have to leave her home in fear. She's been so excited and happy about the hotel, and now that's come to a halt."

"Yes, you're right about that." She sighed. "Very well. I'll tell you what I know. Jenny's mother went to New York to see her and when she came back, she was devastated. Then, apparently, she told one of her friends about the baby, and it got out somehow. You know how bad news goes. Jenny never came home. Illegitimacy wasn't tolerated in those days, and unfortunately, in these cases, the child often suffered more than the parents. Besides, Annie Simon said Forrest had denied the child was his. So there were ugly rumors implied. It's no wonder Jenny never came home. Annie either quit her job at Pennington House or was let go. Finally, she moved away, too. Everyone assumed she'd gone to live with Jenny, but as far as I know, she never contacted anyone in Cedar Chapel again."

I shoved down the sympathy that rose in me for the young Jenny Simon. I couldn't allow myself to be sidetracked by pity.

"But don't you see?" I jumped up from the sofa. "That

makes it even more suspicious that she'd return here."

"I don't know." She closed her eyes and sighed. "It does seem strange. But perhaps she was homesick and wanted to spend her last years where she'd spent her childhood. That's all I know, Victoria. I'm tired, and I need to go to bed."

I thanked her and said good night. When I stepped into the hallway, Miss Simone was passing by on her way to her suite. She gave me a short nod and walked on. Had she heard us? Surely not. She'd have had to be standing with her ear next to the door. I needed to stop seeing trouble in every incident.

I went downstairs to see if anyone needed anything. Frank and Martin were in the rec room, watching a western movie. I found Miss Jane and Miss Georgina sitting on the wicker chairs on the front porch, a pot of tea and a plate of cookies on the table between them.

"You two are turning into regular night owls."

"We are, aren't we?" Miss Georgina giggled then popped a bite of cookie into her mouth.

"Get a cup and join us," Miss Jane said. "There's plenty of tea in the pot." Her welcoming smile was warm. I never had to worry about Miss Jane disapproving of me. We'd always been kindred spirits.

"I don't think I want anything more to eat or drink, but I'll join you." I didn't like them sitting out here alone at night. I sat down on the porch swing and listened to the two friends chatter about a dance the senior center was hosting later in the month.

"Jane, do you think we should invite Jack Riley?" Miss Georgina's face was pink as she darted a glance at her friend.

A very unladylike snort exploded from Miss Jane's

lips. "Now, don't you go making a fool of yourself over that old man."

"I only meant it might be neighborly," Miss Georgina huffed. "And besides, he's only a few years older than we are."

"Oh yeah?" Miss Jane grinned. "What do you suppose Martin would think of you inviting Jack Riley?"

The sweet lady's plump cheeks flamed. "Now, Jane, you stop that. You know there's nothing between Martin and me. And, anyway, he's a lot younger than I am."

I coughed to keep from joining Miss Jane's burst of laughter.

She wiped her eyes with a tissue. "I don't think two years is 'a lot' at our age."

I thought it was time I came to Miss Georgina's rescue. "I think it would be very nice of you to invite Mr. Riley to the dance, if he's still in town at that time. And I'm sure Martin will understand you're only being thoughtful."

A few minutes later, I carried the tea things in and said good night as the ladies went upstairs.

Martin and Miss Georgina? I would never have imagined it.

Sunday morning, I awoke with an eagerness to worship with the people of my church. Since I'd asked God to lead me, to help me do what I felt He was telling me to do and leave the results in His hands, I'd had a new outlook. Now why hadn't I thought to do that before? I could have saved myself a lot of worry and tension.

I stepped into the dining room to find the table set. Miss Jane and Mabel were placing food on the buffet.

They both smiled when I came in, and Miss Jane tossed a little wave my direction.

"Just who I wanted to see," I said, returning the wave. "My partner in crime solving." I grinned in her direction and headed toward the buffet. Today, I felt like indulging in a hearty breakfast. I filled my plate with bacon, eggs, and a biscuit. Then for good measure, I filled a small bowl with gravy. The gravy, of course, called for a second biscuit.

Miss Georgina and Miss Evalina walked in together.

"Well," Miss Georgina giggled, glancing at my plate. "You do have a hearty appetite this morning."

"I do, indeed."

"And you seem mighty cheerful, too."

"I've decided I've been moping around long enough. It's time to put my trust in God. After all, He's the One with all the answers."

"Good for you." Miss Evalina gave me an approving smile.

Miss Jane tilted an eyebrow my way, and I winked. She understood. We'd talk later.

Breakfast over, everyone trooped upstairs to get ready for church. I think between us all there were four denominations, but that was okay. We all shared the same faith in God.

Benjamin arrived, and we said good-bye to everyone and left. Our church was a little too contemporary and lively for the seniors, although they had visited a few times for special services.

The pastor's message reinforced my new resolution to trust God, and I walked into the lodge feeling freer than I had since the murder occurred. Miss Jane and I found a moment to ourselves, and she eagerly agreed to go for a drive with me. I told Mabel to let the seniors know Miss Jane was with me. Otherwise, they'd worry.

"Well, watch the sky," she said, frowning. "Storms are headed this way."

"I will."

"Where are we going?" Miss Jane asked as we slipped out to the garage and got into her Caddy.

"Frankly, I have no idea, but I need to clear my head and relax. And I really wanted your company today." Miss Jane was always good company. Fun and a good sport, she could make me laugh even in dark moments. "Who knows? Maybe we'll run into the sheriff and make his day."

"Maybe we will." She grinned as she started the car and pulled out of the garage.

"Where to first?"

I leaned back against the seat. "Surprise me. Let's just drive for awhile. Maybe we'll get some ideas to help us solve the murder at Pennington House. Because, to be honest, I have no idea what to do next."

"I know. I could tell you were frustrated. It's been more than two weeks. We all want the killer caught and Aggie back home."

We rode in silence as the countryside rushed by. I noticed a flock of geese land in a farmer's field. They must have flown down from the north. They'd keep going until they ended up in Louisiana or Florida. Maybe even south Texas. The sky was clear and beautiful. I had no idea where Mabel had gotten her weather report.

I sat up as I realized Miss Jane had turned onto the road leading up to Pennington House. A twinge of unease gripped my stomach. Hadn't I promised Benjamin I wouldn't do this again? And maybe I had promised God, too.

"Are you sure this is a good idea? Someone got killed here, remember?"

"Oh, so what? We don't have to get out. I just thought maybe we'd get some inspiration from the scene of the crime."

A niggling sense of excitement rose up and pushed out the unease. Also the feeling of guilt.

"Good idea. After all, we solved a crime here once before." Of course, we almost got ourselves killed as well, but I pushed that thought away, too.

"My thoughts exactly." She gave an emphatic nod and threw me a smile.

She pulled up in front of the mansion, and the first thing I noticed was the absence of police tape.

"Do you see what I see?" Miss Jane's voice rang with excitement, and she was out of the car as fast as I was. So much for staying in the car. But surely if the sheriff thought there was any danger, he wouldn't have removed the warning tape. And we'd be very careful.

We were halfway to the front porch when I heard a noise coming from the rear of the house. Miss Jane and I glanced at each other, and without a word, we both rushed around the side of the house. A flash of red was just disappearing into the woods. By the time we'd crossed the vast expanse of the back lawn and reached the edge of the trees, no one was in sight.

"Well, fiddlesticks," Miss Jane exclaimed. I knew how she felt.

"Where do these woods lead?" Maybe we could drive around and cut off the trespasser before he could get away.

"Just further up the mountain." She frowned. "There used to be an old logging road somewhere up there, but I have no idea how to find it. And I can't even remember where it comes out." The sound of exasperation that emitted from her lips affirmed her frustration.

"It's all right. Chances are, he's long gone anyway."

"Do you think we should tell Bob Turner?"

"Probably. But I doubt it'll do any good. We won't be able to identify the guy. In any case, I'd like to look around, first. Maybe we can find out why he was prowling about the place."

We turned and headed for the rear of the house. The back door was padlocked and didn't appear to have been tampered with. We went all around the house, checking doors and windows.

"This window is wide open." Miss Jane's voice sounded more indignant than fearful as she pointed to the opening. I stepped over and peered through the window, but the darkness inside didn't reveal anything. I reached up and slid the window closed.

We walked around to the front and climbed the stone steps to the front porch and sat on the wicker rockers that Miss Aggie had placed there. The cushions had been removed, but the chairs were comfortable.

Miss Jane leaned back and sighed. "It's like going back more than a half century." Nostalgia was written all over her face. "Aggie and I spent a lot of time out here, talking about boys and carrying on as girls tend to do." A shadow clouded her eyes. "Of course, a lot of her schemes were cooked up here, too."

I knew from things she'd told me that Aggie Pennington Brown had had a cruel streak when she was younger. Especially when she was deprived of something she wanted. But she was an old woman now, and she didn't deserve the troubles she'd been through this past year or so.

"I wish she'd come home." Miss Jane's voice trembled, and I reached over and patted her hand.

"She will, soon." I stood. "Well, we might as well leave, I guess."

She sprang out of the chair. "Aren't we going to look inside?"

"Do you think we should?"

"Of course. Whoever was here is long gone now. And we need to lock that window."

"You have the key with you?"

"Yes. I keep it on my key chain."

I laughed. "Well, then. Let's not waste any more time. Lead the way."

Miss Jane turned the key and pushed the heavy door open. We stepped inside.

"Miss Jane, do you know where the tunnel entrance is where the body was found?"

"Aggie said it was in the old kitchen."

"Old kitchen?"

"Yes, when the house was built, the kitchen was separate from the main house and a covered walkway ran between them. That way, the heat from cooking couldn't get into the house in the summer. You know, they didn't have air-conditioning back then. Matter of fact, we didn't have air-conditioning when Aggie and I were growing up, either." She fanned her face with her hand. "How in the world did we stand it?"

The house was rather hot and muggy. How *did* they

stand it back then? I suppose if you were used to it. . .still, I could understand the kitchen being separate.

"But later the walkway was enclosed, and they turned the old kitchen into a utility room. Funny how we still call it the old kitchen. Anyway, that's where they found the entrance to the second tunnel."

"I think I'd like to check it out."

"I agree. After all, when we went through the library and the secret room, we barely made it inside before the sheriff caught us."

Miss Jane led the way through the huge, newly remodeled kitchen, shiny with stainless steel appliances and counters. We walked down a long hallway, then Miss Jane opened a door, and we stepped into the utility room.

The room was bare of any furnishings; electrical wiring stuck out from every wall. A side wall had been partially torn down.

"And there it is," Miss Jane breathed the words, a look of awe on her face. Through the torn-out mess, another wall had been built, and a small door stood open.

I reached out my hand and stopped Miss Jane, who had started forward.

"Don't you think the sheriff would have locked that door?"

"Oh! You're right." Her voice was shrill in the empty room, and she must have noticed it, because her next words were almost a whisper. "Do you think someone is here?"

"No, but I think he was here, and I think he opened the tunnel door. He must have heard us coming up the hill, and that's when he bolted."

I took one timid step and stopped.

I glanced at Miss Jane, who looked as nervous as I felt.

"Well, we're not going to find anything, just standing here. Are you okay to go, Miss Jane?"

"Of course. No dark, dank, spider-filled tunnel can scare me." A slight tremor in her voice belied the brave words, which raised my admiration for her even more.

I reached over and took her hand, stiffened my back, and we walked toward the door together.

My skin felt clammy as we crept down the musty-smelling tunnel, and we hadn't gone five feet before we noticed a decrease in the lighting. If only we'd brought a flashlight. But, of course, we didn't know we were coming here. We walked almost at a snail's pace. I felt something brush my face and reached up, swatting with my hand. Cobwebs clung to me.

A spitting, coughing sound came from behind me.

"What's wrong? Are you okay?"

"Ugh. Just a mouthful of cobwebs. I'm all right now."

Once more, we started down the tunnel.

Suddenly, I noticed a change in the feel of the ground beneath my feet.

"Victoria," Miss Jane's whisper echoed hollowly in the empty tunnel. "I think the floor is wet."

I dug the toe of my shoe into the dirt. "You're right. It almost feels like mud."

"What in the world. . . ?"

"Hold on to my belt, okay? We don't know what we're looking for."

"All right." I felt a tug at my waist as she grabbed the leather. "I don't recall Bob or Tom mentioning this dampness, do you?"

"No. But they don't tend to tell us much anyway."

"No, they sure don't." She gasped. "Do you feel that wind?"

Cool air caressed my face. Or perhaps *caress* wasn't the right word. It felt more like the brush of cold, clutching fingers.

"Yes, I feel it, and that doesn't make sense, does it?" The other entrance to the tunnel ended in the secret room. There wouldn't be any air coming from there. "I think maybe we've veered off the main tunnel. But no one said there was another branch to it, did they?"

"Not that I heard." Her voice, so nervous a moment before, trilled with excitement. I grinned. Sleuths on the trail.

"Well, this tunnel has to end somewhere. Do you want to keep going, or would you rather go back?"

"Go back?" Indignation colored her tone.

I chuckled. "Okay, let's keep going, but don't let go of my belt."

"I won't." Another tug assured me she'd gripped it more tightly.

We continued down the dank tunnel, which seemed to go on and on. To be honest, I was beginning to get a little nervous. How long had we been in here? My feet were aching.

"Miss Jane? Do you want to turn back? I know you must be tired because I am."

I heard her take a deep breath. "Let's go a little bit farther. If we don't reach the end, we'd better turn back. It seems like we've been walking for miles."

"Wait, it's getting lighter, and I think the tunnel is widening." Then with no warning, we found ourselves in a large room. The dirt walls and floor were hard packed.

"Well, I'll be." Miss Jane's awe matched my own.

Wood pallets were stacked up on one side of the room. And others were scattered haphazardly about. Rocks of varying sizes were piled up in one area. In another wall, an opening sloped slightly upward. Sunlight filtered through.

"It's a cave," Miss Jane said, seating herself on a stack of pallets. Her words were matter-of-fact, and I had no reason to question them. After all, she grew up around here and was familiar with the local terrain.

"It seems to be some sort of warehouse," I mused. "But who could have put it to such a use, and what in the world did they store here?"

"Nothing legal, I'll bet." Miss Jane's voice sounded as though it came through clenched teeth. "Maybe there was truth in the rumors about the Pennington wealth, after all. Maybe the old man really was involved in shady dealings." I knew she was speaking of Aggie's father.

"I don't know, Miss Jane. We may never know. But I don't think these pallets are over a hundred years old."

"Oh. Of course they're not. But they do look rather old." She got up, groaning, and dusted off the back of her slacks.

"Well, let's see where we are." I walked across the room and stepped up through the opening, with Miss Jane right behind me.

"Why, we've come out at the river!" Miss Jane exclaimed. "Listen."

We stood in a thick copse of trees and couldn't see anything beyond, but I could hear the rushing of water nearby.

I turned and looked at the opening. It appeared to be six or seven feet wide. But embedded in an embankment and surrounded with trees and bushes, no one would have seen it unless they knew exactly where to look.

Clouds had begun to gather while we were inside, and a roll of thunder sounded in the distance. The storm was coming our way.

I hurried after Miss Jane, who was making her way through a forest of ancient oak and cedar trees. We burst out of the woods.

I stood, staring at the river as it rushed by. And my mind began to whirl with possibilities. I wasn't sure who, what, or when. But the evidence now pointed strongly to some sort of smuggling activities. Was the smuggling just a crime from the past, totally unrelated to the present? Or could it be connected to the Pennington House murder?

Back at the lodge, we all sat huddled in the small, front parlor while the storm raged. Miss Jane was exhausted after our adventure, and I had a few aches myself. It didn't help that the electricity had been off for nearly an hour. I'd gathered all the candles I could find, so light danced in the shadows of the room. We'd built a fire, more for comfort than warmth, although the air had cooled quite a bit as afternoon turned into evening.

A reluctant Mabel had joined us only after I'd insisted. She'd had every intention of braving the storm in order to go home to her aging Persian cat, Goldy.

"Let's sing a hymn," Miss Georgina suggested. "Perhaps it will make us all feel better."

"Good idea." I nodded in agreement and noticed the rest of the group seemed to cheer up a little, too, as Miss Georgina went to the piano and opened the lid.

Everyone, that is, except Miss Simone, who sat rigidly in her chair with a sour expression on her face.

"Don't you like hymns, Miss Simone?" I asked, curious to know one more thing about the elusive actress.

"I don't really see what good they accomplish," she said stiffly.

"They always bring me a great deal of comfort," Miss Georgina said, with a shocked expression on her face.

"I don't need comforting." Miss Simone snapped the words, almost ferociously.

Surprised, I watched her from the corner of my eye as the rest of us began to sing. Her lips were pressed together tightly, and she clutched the scarf at her throat. I thought I knew why. Miss Simone probably didn't have a relationship with God. I decided to talk to her about it the first chance I got. That is, if she'd let me.

We sang a number of traditional hymns and a few more contemporary choruses. The storm continued and showed no signs of letting up.

The phone in the hall rang. I was glad I had kept a couple of corded telephones. The cordless phones, of course, weren't working.

It was Benjamin, checking to see if we were all right.

"We're fine, Ben. You're not out in this, are you?"

"No, I'm holed up at Perkins'. They have a small generator, so we have coffee. Not much else."

I groaned. "Lucky. Coffee sounds wonderful."

"Aw. Sorry, sugar. But the power should be back on any minute."

"If it stops before it gets too late, come over. Miss Jane and I uncovered something today. We haven't told the others yet. It's been too hectic here."

"What is it?"

"Nope. You'll have to wait." I wasn't about to tell him on the phone. He'd probably be so angry he wouldn't come over.

"Fine. Be like that. Okay, see you later."

I knew his reporter antenna would be on the alert. That is, if he took me seriously. Sometimes he didn't.

I dialed Corky's cell phone. He needed to know what was going on at Pennington House. After three rings, it went to his message line. I left a short message and hung up.

An hour later, the power came back on. Miss Simone went upstairs, and Frank and Martin went to the rec room to watch a movie.

"Miss Storm, do you want me to make tea before I leave?" Mabel's voice sounded worried, so I knew I needed to send her home.

"No, don't bother; I know you're anxious to get home to Goldy. I'll take care of it, Mabel."

She gathered her things and left, reminding me that the next day was Monday, her day off. But she left a roast, seasoned and ready to pop into the oven. And there were apple pies for dessert.

"All right, you two." Miss Evalina leveled a glance at me then switched it to Miss Jane. "I know you're up to something. You've been giving each other 'looks' all evening."

"We do have some news," I admitted. "I was waiting until Benjamin arrives, so I can tell you all together."

"Very well, then let's have that tea while we wait."

"Sounds good to me." I went to the kitchen and set the kettle on. While I waited for the water to boil, I prepared a tray with muffins, cream, and sugar.

Benjamin arrived just in time to carry the tray into the parlor. I went upstairs and tapped on Miss Simone's door.

"Yes?"

"I made tea. Would you like for me to bring you some?"

"No, thank you. I'm getting ready for bed."

"Oh. Good night then." A little early for bed. But Miss Simone often retired early.

When I walked into the parlor, Benjamin scooted over and made room for me on the love seat. Frank and Martin left their movie in favor of banana muffins and were laughing, most likely at one of Benjamin's jokes. I didn't bother to ask.

I took a sip of hot Darjeeling and leaned back. "You tell them, Miss Jane."

Her face brightened. "Well, all right, if you're sure."

She leaned forward, her eyes bright. "Victoria and I went to Pennington House today. And we found the other entrance to the tunnel wide open—you know, the one from the old kitchen, where they found the body."

She paused for effect, and when it was obvious she had everyone's attention, she continued.

"The tunnel was dark and creepy. And I couldn't wait to get to the other end where the secret room was. But we never made it."

She looked around the room. "Because we ended up in another branch of the tunnel. It was even worse than the first. Cobwebs clutched at us from the ceiling and walls, and it seemed to go on forever."

A gasp from Miss Georgina interrupted her tale. Miss Jane grinned and continued.

"Suddenly, we felt wind on our faces. That's when we realized we were in a different section of the tunnel."

As she paused again, Martin gave an impatient snort. "Dang it, Jane, stop the foolishness and get on with the story."

She tossed him an indignant look then quickly related the rest of the events.

"A cave no one knew about?" Martin looked shocked. "I thought I knew all the caves around here."

"Well, apparently someone knew about it," said Benjamin. "I wonder how long it's been since the shenanigans went on."

I stared at him. Wasn't he going to yell or anything? After all, I had broken a promise, hadn't I?

"You need to tell the sheriff about this." Miss Evalina was frowning. She knew the trouble we'd had with Bob Turner before, but I knew she was right.

"Actually, Miss Jane and I planned to give him a call when we got home, but then the power went out." I sighed. "I think maybe we should wait until morning. I don't know about the rest of you, but I don't feel like dealing with him tonight."

"Wouldn't surprise me any if he already knows about it." Sometimes Martin was very astute.

There seemed to be a general agreement. Benjamin left, and the seniors all trailed upstairs. I cleaned up the tea things and went to bed shortly afterward. It had been a long, exciting day.

The next day, bright and early, Miss Jane and I went to the sheriff's office. He looked pained to see us, as usual. As we'd suspected, Sheriff Turner didn't appear surprised to hear about the third tunnel, but he did perk up with interest when we told him about the open window and the person we'd seen running away. He thanked us for the information, and we left.

"Victoria, didn't you think he would say something about us intruding on the scene of the crime or something?"

"I think they must be finished there. After all, the crime-scene tape was gone."

"That's right. I forgot."

"I'm going to stay downtown for a while, Miss Jane. I'll walk home later."

"You're sure? I don't mind waiting for you."

"No, I think the walk will feel good today."

She got into her Caddy and pulled away from the curb, tires squealing.

The aroma wafting from the Mocha Java was too tempting to pass up this time, so I went inside and sat at the counter, where I placed my order. The tall caramel latte tantalized my senses. I took my time, enjoying every sip, then left. I stood outside the door of the coffee shop, inhaling the clean air. There was something about the air after a storm.

I went to Millie's Beauty Salon and made an appointment for the following week for the works. Bob Turner's wife was there having her nails done.

"Hi, Victoria." Her eyes crinkled when she smiled. "I saw you and Jane Brody leaving the courthouse. Were you giving my poor husband a hard time again?"

I grinned. Sherry Turner had a great sense of humor. She had to, being married to Bob.

"Yeah, trying to. But this time, he was too nice. He must be up to something."

She laughed. "You're probably right."

I waved and left the salon. I turned left and headed

down the sidewalk, taking my time. As I neared the bank, I noticed Miss Simone standing at the end of the block. She was talking to someone, but the corner building obstructed my view. I ducked into the recessed area before the door of the bank and watched. Miss Simone spoke with animation and seemed agitated. Suddenly, she turned and hurried across the street. Her car was parked by the curb, and she got in and drove off. I hurried the few steps to the side street and rushed around the corner. Whoever she'd been talking to was gone.

I walked home, deep in thought. Was it time for me to confront Miss Simone? Probably not. But I could at least question her about today. And about the phone calls. Maybe someone was just harassing her. She could be totally innocent of all my suspicions.

There I went again. *Calm down, Victoria. You've given this to God. Remember?*

When I got home, I was surprised to find that Miss Simone hadn't returned. I'd assumed she was on her way home. A little niggling of worry tugged at my stomach. I brushed it aside. After all, she had a life.

I was in my office when I heard her come in. It was almost time for lunch, so I decided to wait until later to talk to her.

Lunch was a delicious shrimp salad, vegetable soup, and hot croissants. Miss Simone talked quietly to Miss Jane and me. The rest of the seniors were at the center. Miss Simone seemed in a rare good mood, which surprised me after what I'd seen earlier.

By the time lunch was over, I'd chickened out. I didn't want to rile her up when she was behaving so civilly.

When I passed her room a little later, I heard the

shrilling of a cell phone and paused.

I started to walk on when I heard her voice raised. "Why can't you just drop this insanity? Leave this place while you still can." A pause, then she continued. "No, you have to stop this. If you don't. . .if you don't. . .I may go to the authorities."

She must have hung up the phone because great, racking sobs were the only thing I heard after that. It was time. Whether Miss Simone was involved in something illegal or was an innocent victim, I had to talk to her.

Taking a deep breath, I tapped on her door.

13

I heard her gasp. The sobbing stopped instantly.

"Yes. Who is it?" The words were choppy. Angry.

Maybe I'd made a mistake. I hesitated, wondering if I should slink silently into the shadowy hallway and up to my room. But no. I was trying to be led by God in this, and I felt strongly that I was supposed to talk to her.

Taking a deep breath, I planted my feet. "It's Victoria. May I come in?"

Footsteps crossed the floor, and the door opened a crack. Miss Simone's face looked ravaged as she squinted at me, making no move to ask me in.

"Please, Miss Simone. I need to talk to you."

A look of resignation crossed her face. Slowly, she opened the door and stepped back, motioning me to enter.

Miss Simone's room was as neat as a pin. I'd just given it a good cleaning on Friday. Most of the seniors preferred to make their own beds each morning. But Mabel or I took care of Miss Simone's.

"What do you want to speak to me about, Victoria?" She didn't offer me a chair, so I figured I'd better get to the point.

"I heard you crying as I passed your door. I wanted to make sure you were all right."

"As you can see, I'm fine. Now, is there anything else?"

I was tempted to say no and make my escape, but I pulled some courage out of somewhere.

"Miss Simone, I believe someone is harassing you in some way. The phone calls, your tears. . .and today, I saw you on the square in an argument with someone."

Fear glazed her eyes, and she started breathing heavily. "Who? Who did you see me arguing with?"

"I didn't see who it was. Why don't you tell me? I want to help you, if you'll let me."

Relief washed over her face, and she attempted a laugh.

"You must have seen me speaking to the little boy who almost ran me over. He was skateboarding on the sidewalk."

Could it be true? If so, I'd just made a fool of myself. But I wasn't buying it.

"I didn't hear a skateboard."

"Are you calling me a liar?"

"Of course not. But I think you're afraid of something, and for some reason, you're also afraid to tell anyone."

"Well, my dear, you have quite an imagination. I appreciate your concern, but I assure you there is nothing wrong."

"Then why have you been crying?"

She swallowed, and panic appeared on her face. Quickly, she composed herself.

"A friend of mine passed away recently. We were close. I'm sorry if my tears caused you concern." She opened the door and stood beside it, pointedly waiting for me to leave.

Which I did.

I didn't believe her for a minute, but what could I do? Keep watching.

I knelt beside my bed. *Lord, I'm trying to do only what*

I feel You're telling me to do. If I'm mistaken about Miss Simone, please let me know.

"Corky, I've been trying to get in touch with you. Didn't you get my message?"

"Sorry, I forgot to check messages until this morning."

"Miss Jane and I went to Pennington House a couple of days ago."

"I know. The sheriff told me about the intruder and about the cave. I wonder if Aunt Aggie was aware of it."

"Who knows? She's not one to reveal things about her family. Especially if she thinks it'll make her father look bad. Come on in. We're about to sit down to lunch."

"Actually, I'm on my way out of town. I'm picking up Jack Riley in about ten minutes."

"Jack Riley?"

"Yes. He's very interested in viewing some of the Pennington heirlooms. So far, Aunt Aggie has flatly refused to let him see them for some reason. But she has agreed to speak with him. I think she's just curious. But I agreed to take him to Jefferson City to meet with her."

"Has she mentioned anything about returning home? We all miss her."

"I know. So do I. The sheriff has finally given his okay for the crew to get back to work. We'll be back in business tomorrow, so I'm hoping Aunt Aggie won't be able to stay away much longer." He chuckled. "You know how she likes to be in the thick of everything."

"Oh yes. That she does."

I thought of the crew returning to work the next day. But we hadn't really had a chance to search the tunnels for clues. What if the sheriff had missed something?

"Corky, would you mind if we take a last look at the tunnels before your crew gets back to work?" Once the work crew started on the place, any clues would be obliterated.

"Hmm. I don't know. There's still a killer running loose around here somewhere."

"If I promise to take Benjamin?"

"Okay, if you promise."

I waved as his SUV pulled away from the curb.

Not wanting to break another promise, I picked up the phone, dialed Benjamin's number, and was relieved when he answered.

"Hi, it's me."

He laughed. "I do have caller ID, you know."

"Oh. I forgot. Fine. Don't be a smart aleck. I need to talk to you about something."

He laughed again. "Okay, talk away. I'm always here for you."

"No, I don't want to talk on the phone."

"Okay, I'll be right over." Precious Benjamin. He truly was always there for me.

"Not yet. The gang are all at the center. And they'll have fits if I leave them out. They'll be home around one. Could you come then?"

"Sure, no problem. Are you sure you don't want to give me an idea of what's going on?"

"I'm sure. See you later—and thanks."

I hung up. I still couldn't figure out why he was being so nice. Had he finally realized I could take care of myself?

Then a disturbing thought crossed my mind. Could he have given up and decided he didn't care anymore?

Oh, there went my imagination again. Of course Benjamin cared. Shaking off the doubt, I headed to my office to do some work on the computer. But my restless thoughts grabbed on to Corky's trip to Jefferson City.

So, Jack Riley was interested in Pennington heirlooms. Maybe even the emeralds? Once more, suspicion raised its head, and I shook it off quickly. I wasn't going there again.

My intentions were good, but when I sat behind the desk, I remembered my notebook was in the top drawer. I took it out and looked over what I had.

> *Victim: Who was he?*
> *Fact #1: Elderly man, approximately the age Robert Brown would be if he were alive.*
> *Fact #2: The face and body of person buried as R.B. were disfigured, making a positive identification more difficult at that time.*
> *Cause of Death:*
> *Fact #1: A blow on the back of the head with the rock?*
> *Fact #2: Could not have been an accident, due to position of blow.*
> *Motive: Possibly something to do with missing Pennington emeralds? But, if they came up missing when Mr. Pennington was alive, Robert Brown wouldn't have been in the picture.*
> *If, on the other hand, they came up missing on the day R.B. was supposedly killed—did he fake his death and run off with the emeralds? But then,*

why would he have come back? Did he hide them in the tunnel? But then, why did he wait so long to try to retrieve them?

Possible Suspects:

Jeannette Simone. Find out if there is anything in her past to shed light on her actions.

Keep an eye on her activities, and try to find out who she sees, if anyone, outside the lodge.

Talk to Miss Jane.

Why would a wealthy, retired actress choose to return to Cedar Chapel?

Why would a wealthy, retired actress choose to live at the lodge?

Did Miss Simone hold anger against the Penningtons because of the way Forrest treated her?

Could she possibly be so bitter that she'd resort to murder?

And what was Miss Jane holding back?

What if it was true that Miss Simone had a motive other than revenge?

Who did she talk to on the phone that upset her so? Could there be an accomplice?

Why was she suddenly so interested in the progress of the murder investigation?

Was Forrest the father of her child, and did she think that child deserved part of the Pennington wealth?

Who was she arguing with on the street?

Clyde Foster. Friend/follower of Forrest Pennington? (Hero worship?)

Had a bad temper.
According to Miss Jane, he was very cruel
when they were young.

I sat tapping my pen against my teeth. So far, I'd focused mostly on Miss Simone. But really, the only reason was because of the possible connection between her and Forrest. I didn't honestly believe Miss Simone was a murderer or an accomplice to a murder, but I couldn't throw aside the possibilities.

As for Clyde, my assumptions were mostly based on my dislike for the man.

What about Jack Riley? Should I put him on the list? I tossed the notebook and paper in the drawer. Jack Riley's name wasn't on it.

I went to the kitchen and made a salad and sandwiches for Miss Simone and me. The other seniors were, as usual, at the center. After lunch, she went into the rec room. A few minutes later, the television blared, then almost immediately, the sound was lowered. At least she wasn't holing up in her room, as she usually did.

Benjamin pulled up in front just as Frank's truck followed Miss Jane's Caddy into the garage.

I had iced tea and coffee waiting in the parlor. When the seniors found out what was going on, they all filed in, curiosity written on each face.

"Hey, Ben, what did you think of Victoria and Jane sneaking off to Pennington House?" Martin's excited words banged into my consciousness.

Shoot, I should have known I wouldn't get off so easily. This was the moment Ben would explode.

Miss Jane shot Martin an angry look then turned to

Benjamin. "It was really my fault. Don't you be getting mad at Victoria." Miss Jane, my champion.

"It's all right, Miss Jane. I won't be mad." Benjamin threw me a smile. "I promised to trust her, and I do."

A rush of love washed over me, and I gave him a grateful look. He hadn't forgotten. That's why he was being so nice.

"Oh. Well, it was still my fault. We were going for a drive, and I decided to go to Pennington House."

Benjamin wrinkled his brow. "I still don't understand how the cave could have remained undiscovered all these years."

"That's what I said," Martin put in.

"It would be easy enough to keep it hidden if someone put their mind to it," Frank said with conviction. "And through the years, I suppose the natural growth of trees and brush kept it covered."

"You're probably right." Ben turned to me. "So what do you have in mind? I know you didn't ask me over here to discuss what you've already been up to."

"Corky stopped by this morning on his way out of town. They're going to start back to work on Pennington House tomorrow." I took a sip of iced tea. "I'd like to go over the cave and the tunnels thoroughly before it's too late."

"Don't you think the sheriff took care of that little item?"

"Oh, I'm sure he did. And maybe he even found something. He certainly wouldn't tell us if he did." That was the one thing I was sure of. "But there is a chance they may have overlooked something."

"Did you ask Corky for permission? After all, it is his property. Well, his and Miss Aggie's."

"Of course. It's okay with him, as long as you go with me."

Uh-oh. I shouldn't have added that last part.

"I see. That's why you want me to come along."

"Actually, I was going to ask you anyway. I promise." I grinned, and he shook his head and laughed.

———

After dinner, we loaded up and soon were driving up the steep hill to Pennington House, the van purring like a kitten. Larry knew his repair business. Miss Evalina had stayed at the lodge to keep Miss Simone company. When we'd left, they were chatting over a game of cards.

I pulled up in front of the porch steps, and we stepped out of the van and into the darkness. We'd come with plenty of flashlights. Benjamin had brought his toolbox, so I felt we were prepared for anything.

Miss Jane unlocked the front door, and we stepped into the vast hall. The power was on in this part of the house, so Miss Jane flipped a switch. I think we all breathed a sigh of relief. There's something creepy about a dark house. Any dark house. And we had especially bad memories connected with this one.

"Should we go back outside and check the cave first?" asked Martin.

"I hate to walk all that way in the dark." Miss Jane was right. The cave was at least a mile from the house, probably more. I was surprised Miss Jane was willing to walk so far again, this soon.

"Let's go this way," I said. "We can start from the secret room and see if we can find the intersecting tunnel from this direction. Besides, we never did get a chance to search the room."

"Okay, someone lead the way. I wasn't with you either time, remember?" Benjamin shot a glance my way, but I could see he was teasing.

Frank led the way to the library and through the hidden door. We walked down the plush, carpeted hallway and into Mr. Jason Pennington's secret room. I stopped just inside, savoring an unexplainable ambience. Even in the darkness, with the lights from the flashlights darting in the shadows, this place radiated wealth. Wealth that few people knew today. Even the rich and famous. Somehow, this was different. A lingering, haunting memory of a time gone by.

Benjamin and the seniors were already busy combing the room. I walked to the massive desk, and after brushing the dust off the leather chair, I sat down and started opening drawers.

I don't know what I expected to find, but disappointment washed over me when I realized the desk was empty. I attempted to lift a corner of the old-fashioned green blotter, but it seemed to be glued on. I tugged, and it came loose. It had just been stuck. Running my hand over the wooden surface, I reached all the way under the blotter up to my elbow. My heart raced as my fingers touched something. Carefully, I pulled. And stared at the piece of yellowed paper in my hand.

The ink was faded, and in the darkness, the letters were unreadable. I folded the paper and shoved it deep into my jeans pocket. I'd have to examine it when we got back to the lodge.

"Vickie, there doesn't seem to be anything here. Shall we search the tunnel?"

I stood and joined the others as Frank opened the door to the tunnel.

As I stepped through the doorway, the feeling of claustrophobia returned. Why was it so much worse from this entrance than from the other end? *Because when you were in the other one, you could only feel the chilling cobweb fingers, but this section feels like a tomb.*

I laughed, but it sounded more like someone choking.

"Victoria, are you all right?" Benjamin was at my side.

I took a deep breath. What was wrong with me? I'd never been a coward. What was it about this place?

"I'm fine, Ben. Let's go." And I pushed through the cobwebs.

14

The closed-in feeling began to lift as we walked down the shadowy corridor. Light from the flashlights danced across walls and ceiling, revealing more cobwebs and nothing else.

"Benjamin, wait." He stopped, and the rest of us stopped behind him. "If there's anything here, we're going to miss it if we just walk down the tunnel. Shouldn't we be examining the walls and the floor?"

He looked at me for a second then laughed. "I guess I'm not much of a sleuth, am I?"

"That's okay, Benny," Miss Jane piped up. She reached past me and patted him on the arm. "Victoria and I are. Just do what we do."

The whole gang burst into laughter. Suddenly, any traces of lingering fear disappeared. Our close little huddle split, and we each began to run our flashlights along the walls and floor. When they revealed nothing, we walked a little farther and repeated our actions.

"Everyone, watch for the intersection. It should be veering off soon." I remembered Miss Jane and I hadn't known when we'd changed corridors until we noticed the dampness of the dirt beneath our feet. At least we could see where we were going this time.

"Here it is." Martin's excited statement echoed along the corridor, and every flashlight pointed in his direction.

The tunnel split off sharply from this direction, and I could see how easily we could have followed along coming from the other end without realizing we'd changed corridors. In fact, without the lights, we'd have probably done the same thing now and ended up in the utility room.

We turned and headed down the tunnel that would take us to the cave warehouse.

Suddenly, Miss Georgina stumbled, and I grabbed her arm to prevent her from falling.

"My foot caught on something."

I beamed my flashlight at the floor. At first I could see nothing, so I knelt down and ran my hand over the dirt. My fingers hit a hard lump beneath the damp floor. I began to dig at the sand.

The others had gathered around, and Benjamin knelt down and ran his hand over the object I'd uncovered.

"Frank, would you please look in the toolbox and get me something to dig with."

Frank obliged, handing some strange-looking tool to Benjamin, who started to dig gently around the object.

As Benjamin dug and pushed dirt aside, the artificial light revealed pieces of wood buried beneath the floor.

"Okay." He stopped digging and stood up. "It's some kind of track."

"A track?" I think we all spoke in unison, surprise in every voice.

"But there aren't any railroad tracks around here, Ben." Frank's apparent astonishment was exactly what I was feeling.

"I know." Benjamin glanced around at us. "But I think I know what they are. Let's keep going."

We continued down the corridor, with Ben pausing every now and then to dig, uncovering several more portions of the track. Finally, we made it to the cave.

There was a little more light in here, due to moonlight streaming through the opening, but again, we used the beams from our flashlights to examine the room. Benjamin concentrated on the floor, uncovering more of the wooden track.

"Okay, here's what I think." Benjamin stood and dusted his hands against his jeans. "The track was used to haul things from this cave to Pennington's secret room. They would have had to use some sort of wheeled cart. I suspect we'll find more track leading to the river."

"Then old man Pennington really was involved in something crooked." Frank didn't seem too surprised.

"Maybe. We don't know that for sure. It was a long time ago, and whatever it was could have been totally on the up-and-up. Who knows? Maybe he was storing things in case the Germans took over the country."

He walked over to the cave opening and went through. The rest of us followed. More digging turned up more track, which did lead to the river.

"But if he was smuggling things down to the river, why didn't anyone see?" Miss Georgina's pale blue eyes were wide.

"Probably did their work at night," Martin said with relish. "That's what I'd have done. Especially if they were trying to keep the Nazis from finding out."

"There weren't any Nazis around here, Martin. Don't be silly." Miss Jane lowered her voice. "At least, none that I knew about."

"I think we all need to stop conjuring up theories," I said. "We have no idea what the tracks or the warehouse were used for. And remember, this is Miss Aggie's father we're talking about."

Sober looks appeared on their faces, and Miss Jane nodded. "You're right. We need to think about how it will affect Aggie if it turns out her father was involved in something illegal."

Martin snorted. "She'd love it. Probably put it in a fancy advertisement brochure for the hotel."

I suspected he could be right. Miss Aggie was likely to think it was exciting to have a smuggler in the family, since it was in the past. She'd probably give tours. But still, we needed to stop assuming we knew what had gone on here.

Benjamin wanted to check out the branch of the tunnel leading to the secret room, to see if the track extended all the way to it, so we went inside and backtracked. The track did lead all the way to the door of Mr. Pennington's room.

I noticed Miss Georgina breathing hard. I suspected we were all as exhausted as she sounded. I, for one, felt grimy and looked forward to a shower and clean, soft pajamas.

We headed back to the van. The seniors speculated about our discovery the entire ride home. I sighed. I knew there was no stopping it. I just hoped they'd keep the secret among themselves. It would be so easy for rumors about the Penningtons to start up again.

"We'd better keep this to ourselves." Bless Miss Jane.

I sighed with relief at the murmurs of agreement. I knew wild horses couldn't drag the information from them now.

But we needed to tell Corky and Miss Aggie what we'd discovered. And of course the sheriff needed to know, too. I supposed he should be first.

I went to my room when we got back to the lodge. Eagerly, I took the yellowed scrap of paper from my pocket and held it near the lamp next to my recliner. The faded ink was still hard to make out, but it was a list of some sort. I sat in the recliner and leaned closer to the light.

One Diamond Pendant
One Diamond Bracelet with Gold Scroll
One Ruby Pendant, large stone encir—
Large Pica

The paper was torn at a jagged angle. A list of stolen merchandise? Or something totally innocent? Perhaps part of a list for an insurance company.

I put the paper in the drawer. I'd show it to Ben in the morning and get his opinion.

Ben showed up at nine the next morning. He'd informed the sheriff of our find and said he'd seemed surprised.

I showed him the paper I'd found the night before. He was impressed but agreed there was no way to know what the list was for.

All of us, including Miss Simone, were waiting in the parlor when Corky arrived. Since I'd decided to sort of give Miss Simone the benefit of the doubt, as the saying goes, I'd let her in on the investigation. Besides, if she knew what *we* were up to, it might give us a better chance to see what *she* was up to. If anything, of course. In any case, she'd seemed very interested in what I had to say.

"I don't have much time," Corky said, the minute he

came through the door. "I left the crew in the middle of the utility room. Aunt Aggie wants us to wall the tunnel back up from that end."

"Did she have her talk with Mr. Riley?" I couldn't help being curious about this meeting, even if I had decided to shelve my suspicions of the man.

"Yes. She ran me off, so I have no idea what it was all about. After their visit or meeting or whatever it was, Mother insisted we stay for dinner. I hadn't been home in a month or so. We didn't get back to Cedar Chapel until well after midnight."

"We made a rather interesting discovery in your ancestral home," Benjamin said. He then proceeded to tell him about the tracks in the tunnel that led to the river.

Corky whistled. "And the sheriff didn't know about it?"

"In all fairness to the sheriff, we found it by accident." I couldn't believe I was defending Bob Turner. "I'm pretty sure he knows about the other tunnel and the cave, though."

"I wonder if Aunt Aggie knows anything about it."

"I don't think so," Miss Jane said. "If she'd known something this exciting, I'm almost certain she would have mentioned it. And remember, she didn't even know there was a tunnel leading from the secret room to the old kitchen."

"Or so she said." Martin always pretended to think the worst of everyone, but I'd learned over the past year and a half that he was probably the most tenderhearted of all the seniors.

Corky frowned. He hadn't figured Martin out yet and was very defensive of his great-aunt. She pretty much had him wrapped around her little finger. I could see why she had all the boys flocking to her when she was young. Miss Aggie could still charm when she wished to. And apparently, she wished to charm her great-nephew.

"Okay, I'd better get back to Pennington House. Oh, by the way, Aunt Aggie is thinking about changing the name of the place before we send out brochures." He chuckled. "I wonder what she'll come up with."

He left. Benjamin finished his coffee and said he had to get to work also. The seniors headed out to the center, except for Miss Jane, who said she wasn't in the mood, and Miss Simone, who said she had errands to run.

I stared out the window as Miss Simone pulled out of the drive. Maybe I'd made a mistake by opening up to her. Shoving the thought aside, I pushed the cart with the coffee things to the kitchen and discussed the week's menu with Mabel.

"Corky and Phoebe will be here for dinner on Sunday. Probably Benjamin, too."

"Don't worry. I'll fix plenty." Mabel nodded in satisfaction. The more there were for her to cook for, the better she liked it.

Miss Jane popped into the kitchen with an eager look on her face. "Let's go to lunch today, Victoria."

I suspected she wanted to talk sleuthing. But I didn't mind. Maybe I could talk her into trying the Japanese place over at Caffee Springs. So far, neither Ben nor any of the seniors would go there with me, and who wants to eat alone in a restaurant? Hence, I'd never tried it, either.

"Sounds good to me. Why don't you join us, Mabel?"

"Thanks for the invite, but I don't see any point in

eating in a fancy café when I can cook most anything myself." She shook her head. "I'll just make me a sandwich and eat it here."

Miss Jane and I made plans to leave around eleven. I went to my office and checked e-mail. There was one from my mother.

> *Victoria, my darling girl. I do wish you were here in southern France with me. The food is divine, and I've found some wonderful little knick-knacks for the drawing room. How are things going at the lodge? Have they found the horrible man who killed the transient yet? If not, please be careful. Your father has gone back to Dallas on business. I plan to leave for Scotland tomorrow. Can you believe I've let Hillary St. Ives talk me into accompanying her on a walking tour? I'm going to give it a try. If I don't like it, I'll make an excuse and leave. Your father and I plan to meet in London next week. I'll call you this weekend. Ciao.*

Knickknacks. I laughed. Whatever they were, I didn't doubt she'd paid thousands of dollars for them.

I scrolled down and found one from Dad.

> *Hi, little girl. I hope everything is going well. I've left your mother in France and am resting in my own easy chair in the library at home. I miss you. Maybe I'll run up for a visit while I'm home. Love, Dad.*

Sure, Dad. Fat chance. Oh well, I knew he meant well. Just as Mom did. Their lives were simply too busy to include their daughter. Always had been. I sighed and turned off the computer. I absolutely would not wallow in self-pity. I'd been there before. Too many times. It had been a lot easier, though, when Grandma and Grandpa were alive.

I leaned back in my desk chair and closed my eyes. *Father, I only need You.*

Immediately, a warmth washed over me, and I basked in His presence.

I couldn't believe my luck. Miss Jane had actually agreed to try Japanese. She pulled into the parking lot.

"Isn't that Jenny's car?" Miss Jane craned her neck and looked at the silver Lincoln a few cars down from us.

"Hmm, if it's not, it's one identical to hers. I wonder what errands she had here in Caffee Springs?"

"Who knows? Maybe's she's thinking of buying a house or something."

"Oh well. I guess I need to stop being so nosy."

"Yeah, maybe." She grinned as she got out of the car.

Asian music played softly as we were seated at a small table. We'd opted out of the community dining. The lighting was extremely low, and there was a lighted Japanese lantern in the center of the table.

We placed our orders, and a few minutes later, our server, wearing a traditional Japanese kimono, brought a pot of tea and two tiny cups without handles.

Miss Jane's indrawn breath drew my attention, and I

turned to look in the direction she was staring.

"Don't look," Miss Jane whispered intensely. "Turn back around."

Following her instructions, I turned around, giving her a questioning look. She was looking down at her hands.

"What is it, Miss Jane?"

"Shh. Don't say my name so loud. Knock your napkin off the table, and when you pick it up, turn and look back to your left."

Feeling like an idiot, I nevertheless did as she'd commanded.

Jack Riley sat across from Miss Simone. Their heads were almost together as they spoke to each other.

I sat up. And stared.

Miss Simone glanced in our direction, and a look of consternation crossed her face. She said something to Mr. Riley then snatched up her purse, jumped up from her chair, and hurried out, not passing our table.

Astonished, I turned to look at Jack Riley. He waved then placed some money by his water glass and rose. He walked over to us, smiling.

"Well, Miss Brody and Miss Storm. What a nice surprise. If I'd known you were coming, I'd have invited you to join us."

"Thank you, Mr. Riley. It's nice to see you, too. Would you care to join us?"

"I would love to, but I have an appointment in ten minutes."

"I wasn't aware you were acquainted with Miss Simone." I looked closely into his eyes.

"Yes, Jeannette and I have known each other for many years."

"Oh." I sat and stared, not knowing what else to say.

With a smile and finesse, Jack Riley bowed over my hand then Miss Jane's and left us sitting there, staring dumbly after him.

We turned and looked at each other.

Finally, I found my voice. "Why didn't they say they knew each other when he came to dinner?"

"Jenny wasn't there, remember? She was ill and asked for a tray in her room."

"Well, I refuse to get my suspicions riled up. After all, they both grew up around here. Their meeting is probably perfectly innocent."

"I'm sure you're right. It's probably perfectly innocent." She looked about as convinced as I was.

Our meal arrived in little dishes. The food was delicious, and soon, I almost forgot about Miss Simone and Jack Riley.

We headed back for Cedar Chapel, both deep in thought.

Miss Simone's car was in the garage. When we went inside, there was no sign of her.

I walked into the kitchen. Mabel was peeling hard-boiled eggs.

"Where's Miss Simone?"

"She made a beeline for the stairs when she walked in, and I haven't seen hide nor hair of her since."

"Hmm. Okay. Thanks. Did anyone call?"

She pointed her knife toward the whiteboard by the kitchen phone. "All on there."

I glanced through the messages. One from Phoebe. One from an antique store in Branson. Two from Benjamin.

I went to my office. Phoebe would still be at the bank, so I dialed her cell phone.

"Victoria?" She sounded panicky. "Uncle Jack is in the hospital. He's very sick. They think he's been poisoned. I'm leaving now. Could you please meet me there?"

15

When I pulled into the hospital parking lot, I saw Benjamin's truck parked two places down from Corky's SUV. I slid the van in between them, hopped out, and hit the lock button.

The receptionist sat behind a desk, with earbuds in her ears, keying something into the computer. She looked up and slipped one bud out of her ear.

"Benjamin's down there." She jabbed her head in the direction of the hospital's lone waiting room then continued with her transcribing.

"Thanks, Linda."

My heels tapped loudly on the outdated tiles. Most people opted to go to Springfield or Branson when they needed hospital services, except in the case of emergencies. Therefore, the town didn't see the necessity of spending money on the old building.

Phoebe paced the floor, in obvious distress. Her mother sat with her head bowed. Benjamin and Corky were speaking quietly, their faces unreadable.

I sat on the blue plastic chair next to Benjamin, and he took my hand and squeezed.

"How is he?" I asked.

"We don't really know much. The doctor suspects poisoning. Whether accidental or criminal, I've no idea. We're hoping to hear something soon."

My eyes followed Phoebe as she continued to pace. I caught her eye as she turned, and she came over and dropped down beside me.

"Victoria, why would anyone poison Uncle Jack?" Her eyes swam with tears, and she clutched my free hand.

"Tell me what happened."

"Uncle Jack came to the hospital, complaining of severe cramps and dizziness. He could hardly breathe. They say he collapsed before they could get him to a chair."

"Could it possibly be food poisoning?" I thought of the delicious cuisine I'd eaten, and my stomach churned. I wondered if Jack and I'd had the same thing.

"Dr. Thomas didn't say much. Just that Uncle Jack's symptoms indicate some sort of poison." She gave a little half sob, half sniffle. "He hasn't come back to tell us anything."

Corky came over and sat beside her. Wrapping his arms around her, he held her as she cried. Jack Riley was Phoebe's longtime hero, and when she'd finally met him in person, the hero of her childhood fantasies became a beloved uncle. Possibly he'd taken the place of the father who'd walked out when she was two.

I got up and went to Mrs. Sullivan, kneeling in front her and taking her hands in mine. "Is there anything I can do to help?"

She met my gaze with her tearful one and tried to smile. "Just pray. For Uncle Jack and for Phoebe. She's taking this mighty hard."

"I know. And I'm praying." I squeezed her hands.

"Thank you."

"Would you like for me to get you something? Coffee? Something to eat?"

"Coffee would be nice. Maybe Phoebe would go with you. It might do her good to get out of here for a while."

"I'll see what I can do."

I stood and went back to the others. "I'm going to the Mocha Java to get coffee for Mrs. Sullivan. Does anyone else want anything?"

"Coffee sounds good to me," Corky said.

"Phoebe, would you like to ride along?"

"No, I don't think. . ." She stopped. "Well, okay. I'll go." We walked out to the van and got in.

"Thanks, Victoria." She threw me a tremulous smile.

"For what?"

"For asking me to go with you. I was slowly working myself into a frenzy. I don't want to fall to pieces. I have to be strong for Mom in case. . ." She caught her breath.

"It's all right. I know how much your uncle means to you. Let's hope he'll recover quickly from whatever caused his collapse."

We pulled up to the Mocha Java. A few minutes later, loaded down with coffee and rolls, we got into the van and headed back to the hospital.

Mrs. Sullivan was in the hall speaking with a doctor. Phoebe joined them, and I went into the waiting room where Benjamin and Corky sat staring at the door.

"Do you know anything yet?" I whispered the words, not wanting to disturb the Sullivans as they received information from Mr. Riley's doctor.

Benjamin shook his head. A few minutes later, Phoebe and her mother joined us, their faces ashen.

"The doctor believes Uncle Jack will be all right. They pumped his stomach and started him on fluids right away. If he had waited any longer to come in, he possibly could have died." Phoebe's voice trembled. "The doctor says it definitely wasn't food poisoning. There *is* a possibility it could be an allergy of some sort. But the symptoms indicate arsenic poisoning."

"He's sleeping," Mrs. Sullivan said, with relief in her voice. "The doctor said we might as well go on home. He's promised to call us if there is any change."

I drove myself back to the lodge in a turmoil. What if someone *had* tried to murder Jack Riley? I was already running suspects through my head. Miss Simone, his lunch companion, was at the very top of the list.

—

"Another murderer? Or the same one?" Miss Georgina was very near tears. And I supposed she had a right to be. All the seniors seemed despondent during dinner. And I couldn't pretend to be anything less.

"Let's hope not." Although I suspected it was murder, I still held on to the hope they'd find an allergy as the cause of Jack Riley's illness.

I went to my apartment early, nursing a headache. A hot bubble bath and a couple of aspirins later, I sank into my bed and closed my eyes. Then the thought I'd been fighting back all evening screamed inside my head. *If Jack Riley was poisoned by Miss Simone, then it's my fault. I shouldn't have let my guard down with her.*

—

The next morning, I phoned Phoebe.

She burst into tears. "What if someone really tried to kill Uncle Jack? Who would want my uncle dead?"

Nausea rose in my stomach.

"But he isn't dead. Try to calm down, Phoebe. The

doctors will find out what's wrong. And then they'll know what to do for him. Are you going to work today?"

"No, I've taken a personal day. I can't seem to think straight, and I have a terrible headache. I'm so worried."

We talked for a few more minutes, then I convinced her to go to bed and get some rest.

I dropped onto one of the sofas in the parlor. If it was attempted murder, could it be connected with the first? Or did someone have it in for Jack Riley for other reasons?

I remembered I hadn't returned the call from the antique dealer, so I made a quick phone call to her after breakfast. I'd been searching for a certain type of antique bedroom set for my newly renovated third-floor apartment. The dealer informed me that she'd recently obtained a set that might meet my need.

I was elated when Miss Evalina, our resident expert on antiques, offered to ride along to Branson with me to take a look at the set and offer her advice. This would help me to keep my mind off murders and murderers, as well.

Miss Evalina and I drove out of town and headed down the winding, hilly road to Branson. I didn't know why I avoided this trip so much. The entire drive was decorated with the most beautiful scenery I'd ever seen. Wooded hills and lush green valleys always took my breath away. A chestnut mare grazed in a valley, and nearby, a colt pranced around, chasing something in the air too small for me to identify.

I inhaled deeply and let it out slowly, relaxing for the first time in days.

Miss Evalina glanced at me and smiled. No need for words. She understood perfectly. She'd been blessed to live her entire life amid all this beauty. I smiled back, feeling it deep inside.

The oak bedroom set was everything I'd envisioned. Miss Evalina gave it her seal of approval, so I purchased it on the spot, adding a fee to have it delivered the next day.

"Are you in a hurry, Victoria?"

"No, ma'am. I was about to ask you the same thing. What did you have in mind?"

"Silver Dollar City?" Her eyes sparkled, and I grinned. What was the magic of the place that drew us all in?

"Sure you're up to walking those hills?"

"If I get tired, we can stop at one of the shows."

"Sure. We can grab lunch there, too, if you'd like."

"I most certainly would like." Her face glowed with pleasure. She and I hadn't been anywhere without the others in a long time. A twinge of guilt bit at me. I usually invited Miss Jane because, after all, she and I were kindred spirits.

We managed to find a parking lot near one of the tram stops. We'd only waited a couple of minutes when a tram pulled up and we boarded.

I felt a tremor of pleasure. "When I was a child, riding the tram was my favorite part of Silver Dollar City."

"Yes, I remember how excited you always were when you would tell me about your day. The tram was always the major topic."

"Imagine your remembering that."

"Your grandmother would bring you over to my house for tea, or sometimes we'd sit in her parlor for hours. Just the three of us." Nostalgia crossed her face.

"Yes," I whispered. "I remember. I loved those times. You always put flavored honey in my tea."

"That's right. I made it myself from my aunt Sally's recipe."

The park wasn't at all crowded today. School had started, and most of the visitors on weekdays were older couples or locals just hanging out.

The aroma of kettle corn, fried chicken, and other delicious food items assailed me when we entered the square.

"Ummm. I think it's past our lunchtime, Miss Evalina."

"But it will be well worth the wait. Don't you agree?"

"Absolutely. Do you want to eat now, or wait awhile?"

"Let's wait awhile. We could walk down toward the Dockside and see The Cajun Connection first."

I laughed. "You do know Miss Georgina might never speak to us again?"

"Oh, she'll get over it. Maybe I'll take her one of Cedric's CDs."

"You mean there's one she doesn't have?"

"Hmm. Come to think of it, I'm not sure. We really should stop teasing her about Mr. Benoit. It's merely hero worship. Nothing really wrong with that."

"I know." I wondered if I dared ask Miss Evalina a question that had been roiling around in my head for a long time. I decided all she could do was tell me to mind my own business.

"Miss Evalina."

"Yes, dear?" She was carefully making her way down the paved path, glancing at the open shops we passed.

"Did Miss Georgina or Miss Jane ever have boyfriends?" I knew neither of the ladies had ever married, just like Miss Evalina hadn't, but I knew Miss Evalina's reason. She'd always been in love with Frank Cordell.

For a moment, I thought she wasn't going to answer. I was getting ready to make a fast apology and change the subject when she spoke.

"Georgina is probably the bravest person I've ever met."

I couldn't help the little exclamation of surprise and disbelief.

"I know. You're thinking of the fearful bundle of nerves she displays in her daily life. But in the big story of life, she's a rock." She paused. "I'll tell you her story on our ride back. I don't want to get distracted and trip over something."

"All right. Look, there's the Christmas store. Shall we check it out before we head over to see The Cajuns?"

"That is a wonderful idea. Jane and Georgina never want to go in there until at least November. Personally, I could handle Christmas all year."

I looked at her in surprise. I knew she was usually the first to put holiday decorations in her room and was always available when I began decorating the lodge. But I didn't know she was a Christmas nut like me. So. . .Miss Evalina and I were kindred spirits, too.

The shop sparkled with dozens of trees. Green, silver, gold, red. Each with a different theme.

"Look at the figure skates." I hurried over to the tree decorated with sports ornaments. "There must be twenty pairs of skates on here." I was a figure skating fanatic, although I, personally, had never been on a pair of skates.

"Beautiful. And do you see the angel tree?"

We spent thirty minutes in the store and then hurried over to the Dockside, arriving just as a show was beginning.

The next half hour was a whirlwind of enchantment. The band members' green and gold costumes sparkled and shimmered as they danced, sang, made us roar with laughter at their Cajun humor, and drew us in, making us believe we were a part of them, making us wish we were Cajuns, too. Finally, Cedric Benoit ended the show, almost bringing the house down with a rousing, delightful medley of vocals, accompanied by his magical accordion. We were left wanting more.

We made our way to the merchandise table where Miss Evalina purchased a newly released CD for Miss Georgina. We waved to the performers and left, heading across to a rustic café to eat wonderfully messy barbecue sandwiches.

Soon after, we hopped on a tram, tired but happy.

As we left Branson, I turned to Miss Evalina, wondering if she'd forgotten.

She smiled. "I suppose you want to hear Georgina's story."

"Please, Miss Evalina, unless you think she'd mind."

"No, I would not have offered to tell you if I thought I'd be betraying my cousin."

She paused, as before. "Georgina was a tiny slip of a thing back then. Full of fun and life. And sweet as she could be. Grant Johns thought so, too. He fell hard for her, and when she finally accepted his ring, the two were a joy to behold." She stopped, a faraway look in her eyes.

"The only time I saw Grant angry was when we heard that Hitler had invaded Austria. He had an aunt there, and for a while, she kept him posted on what was going on. Then the letters stopped. Grant's mother was almost frantic when she couldn't get word from her sister. Grant became more and more frustrated. When England declared war on Germany, he kissed Georgina good-bye and went to England to join their army."

Pain shadowed Miss Evalina's face. She took a deep breath. "You know how Georgina was there at my side when Frank left me for Aggie. She worried about me, brought me trays to tempt me to eat when I wouldn't come out of my room. When my ordeal was over, Georgina told us her horrible news. News she'd carried inside during the time she cared for me. Grant's plane was shot down over France and his body never recovered. Her darling would never come home."

I reached over and squeezed her hand, and we rode in silence for some time.

"Well," she said, "that was long, long ago. And Grant Johns went to a happier place."

"Thank you for sharing it with me. I understand Miss Georgina better now."

"And now, about Jane. . ." Her lips tilted upward, and her eyes danced. "Jane was never a flirt like Aggie, but she had her share of beaux. She just never found one she wanted to love, honor, and especially obey."

Our laughter rang out the windows as we continued down the highway.

The minute we stepped in the door of the lodge, I knew something was wrong. Everyone was gathered in the front parlor. Miss Georgina met us at the parlor door, her face filled with consternation.

"It's terrible," she cried. "Phoebe called a little while ago. The lab results are back. It truly was poison. Someone tried to kill Jack Riley."

16

Phoebe stopped by on her way to the hospital the next day and informed us that her uncle was doing much better. Although he was still weak and his vision blurred from time to time, the doctor had declared he was out of danger. He'd also said, at Jack's age, it was a miracle the arsenic hadn't killed him.

"As soon as the lab report came in, they started him on dimercaprol, whatever that is. Then after two or three days, they'll give him something called penicillamine until the arsenic level drops. Victoria! He could be dead. He'll be kept another few days until he's received all the prescribed dosages of both medications."

"Phoebe, dear," Miss Georgina said, "tell your uncle to eat two or three cloves of garlic every day. That will remove any remaining traces of the poison."

"Okay, Miss Georgina." Phoebe didn't sound too convinced. "I don't suppose garlic is going to hurt him."

"Not unless he's a vampire," Martin chortled. When no one laughed with him, he grinned and followed Frank out to his truck. Today was bingo day at the center.

"That man!" Miss Evalina frowned and picked up her purse.

"Never mind him, Phoebe." Miss Jane patted the girl's arm. "He's a little crazy, you know." She waved and followed Miss Evalina and Miss Georgina out the door.

Phoebe and I stared at each other for a moment then burst out laughing.

"He's not really crazy," I assured her. "Just a little bit ornery."

"Are you sure?" She giggled. "I'd better get going. They're calling for thunderstorms sometime today." She waved good-bye and left.

I poked my head into the kitchen and told Mabel I'd be on the third floor if she needed me for anything.

"They'll be delivering my new bedroom set sometime today." I'd had to pay extra to get them to deliver on Saturday, but I wanted to sleep in my new bed tonight.

The rooms, consisting of my grandmother's sitting room and Grandpa's old library plus a renovated full bathroom, would be my new apartment. Many of my grandparents' things had either been given away or stored in the attic. I'd kept the antiques to be placed throughout the lodge. Grandpa's books were sitting proudly in the original built-in bookcases in the great hall except for a few I intended to keep in my new bedroom.

I stood in the doorway, watching the lacy curtains blow gently as a light breeze drifted through the open window. Mentally envisioning the new antique bedroom set, I felt a smile coming on.

At the sound of the doorbell, I hurried downstairs and opened the door for the delivery men. I think I must have aggravated them with my hovering as they carried the heavy pieces up the two flights of stairs. When each item was in its proper place, I thanked them profusely, tipped each generously, and closed the door behind them.

"Mabel, come up and look at the new furniture!" I yelled as I headed back up the stairs.

Mabel came, huffing and puffing behind me, and we stood in the doorway, admiring the room.

"This is something, all right," Mabel said with a nod. "What are you gonna put on that round table?"

I glanced at the small table nestled in one of the corners. I frowned. Mabel was right. It needed something.

"I saw a small Tiffany lamp at Marley's Antiques that would look perfect there." I hated to make another trip to Branson so soon. But I wanted the room to be perfect before I moved in, and I didn't know when I'd get another chance. It couldn't be helped.

I glanced at my watch. I could just about make it there and back before lunch. Hopefully, before the forecasted thunderstorm hit.

Halfway home from Branson, the lamp tucked safely among blankets in the back and my checking account greatly debited, a loud clap of thunder indicated lightning had struck somewhere nearby. I glanced nervously at the darkening sky. Raindrops began to spatter on the windshield, and I turned on the wipers. *Please, God, don't let it get too bad before I'm back home.*

Sheets of rain washed across the windshield, resisting the wipers that scraped furiously against the glass. I lifted my foot off the gas pedal and slowed down.

A sudden slack in the rain revealed a figure running along the side of the road. He turned and held up his hand. Trent. I slowed to a crawl and then stopped. I reached across the bucket seat and opened the passenger door.

"Get in," I shouted.

He jumped into the van and slammed the door, turning to me with a grin. Water ran down his face and dripped from his soaked hair. His tank top and running shorts were drenched, and his tan legs were slick with water.

"Your car's going to be soaked, you know." His mouth quirked into a grimace of apology.

"Going to be?" I retorted then smiled. My heart was racing, and I spoke gruffly to keep my voice from trembling. What was it about this man that made me turn into Jell-O?

"Where can I drip you?" Oops. "I mean, drop you?"

He laughed. "You can drip me at my cabin if you don't mind. My road is about a mile from here."

"Didn't you know it was supposed to rain?"

"Yeah, but I thought I could beat it."

"Me, too." I threw him a rueful smile. "I guess we both have poor judgment."

When he indicated the turnoff to his cabin, I maneuvered the car onto the dirt road and drove about a half mile. His "cabin" turned out to be just that. Logs and all. A rustic cabin in the midst of a grove of oak and cedar trees.

"It's lovely," I whispered breathlessly. Was it the scenery or his nearness that affected me so?

"Yes, lovely." His voice was husky, and his eyes narrowed. He started to lean toward me.

"Well," I said, planning to make a hasty retreat, "I'd better get home."

He sat up straight and grinned. "Sorry, I almost got carried away there. Don't try to drive home in this downpour. Come in and have something hot to drink while you wait out the storm."

"I don't think. . ."

He interrupted. "I promise to be a perfect gentleman. Scout's honor."

"Are you sure you were a scout?"

"No, but I promise I'm honorable."

"Well. . .okay. I think there's an umbrella somewhere in back. No sense in me getting as soaked as you are, right?" I lifted my eyebrows in challenge.

"Right." He hopped out and slid open the back door. An instant later, he was at my window, with the opened umbrella in his hand.

I flung open my door and ducked underneath the umbrella, and we made a dash for the cabin. He yanked open the unlocked door, and we practically fell through the opening, laughing.

⸺

I sat on the sofa in front of Trent's stone fireplace, drowsy, watching the flames dance and crackle. I snuggled my chin further into the warm blanket he'd brought me.

"Okay," he said, poking at the log he'd tossed onto the kindling. "This should be just enough. We don't want to get the room too hot. Just take care of the dampness."

He stood and threw me a smile that made me feel giddy. "Now that the fire is taken care of, I'll go change out of these soaked clothes."

I watched as he headed toward the door. He paused by a small table and threw a quick glance my way. As he passed the table, his hand bumped a framed picture, knocking it over.

I stared at his back as he left the room then looked at the picture which lay facedown on the table. Had he knocked it over intentionally? It seemed so to me. But why?

Alert now, I tried to recall everything I knew about Trent. He was new in town. He was a writer. He was gorgeous. And the only one of those things I actually knew for sure was that he was gorgeous.

Had he, perhaps, failed to mention a wife and children?

Of course, it didn't really matter. I wasn't interested in him, romantically. I was engaged to Benjamin. Guilt stabbed my conscience. I hadn't been thinking of my fiancé for the past half hour.

I glanced at the picture again, squinting my eyes. Maybe I should check it out. I sat up, letting the blanket slip down to my lap.

"Whew. I feel better." Trent stood in the doorway. He looked at me then darted a quick glance at the picture. He stepped over and picked it up.

"Looks like the glass has cracked. I'd better put it away until I can get a new frame." He walked into the bedroom, and when he came back, his hands were empty.

"A wife you didn't mention?" I teased. Let him think I was joking.

Relief crossed his face, and then he laughed. "No, I promise, I'm not married. But you're still engaged. Right?"

"Right." Good. He remembered.

"Shame." He shook his head. "Stay cozy. I'll make coffee."

"Maybe I'd better get going."

"Nonsense. It's still pouring." He winked and went into the kitchen.

He was right about the rain. I could hear it pounding against the roof. Perhaps a little bit of hail, too.

I thought again of the photograph but brushed it aside. It didn't really matter. I'd be leaving in a little while, and I certainly didn't intend to get involved with Trent.

In a few minutes, he was back, carrying two steaming mugs in one hand and a plate piled high with donuts in the other.

His hand brushed mine as he handed me the coffee.

I caught my breath and then counted to ten. Why did this man have such an effect on me? I was in love with Benjamin. Steeling myself against my raging emotions, I took a sip of the hot liquid. A little strong for me, but at least it was hot.

By the time we'd finished our coffee, the rain had slowed down a lot, so I decided it was high time for me to leave.

"Well, thank you for the coffee and the fire." I set the cup on the table and got up. "I'd better get home now."

Trent stood and walked me to the door. He had that look in his eye again, so before he had a chance to do whatever he was thinking, I thrust my hand at him.

He smiled and took it gently in his. "Until the next stormy day, then."

Not likely. I headed home with a sigh of relief. *Next time I'm caught in a storm, I'll take my chances on the road.*

I glanced at my watch as I pulled into the garage at home: 11:55. Just in time for lunch.

———

I spent all afternoon moving my things into the new apartment. I put my own sheets and down comforter and pillows on the oak four-poster bed and patted the familiar bedding with satisfaction. Now it was truly my bedroom and not Grandpa's library. A twinge of regret bit at me, and I glanced at the corner bookcase that held a set of leather-bound classics. Grandpa's favorites. The only bit of nostalgia I'd allowed to remain in the room. Life goes on, and I refused to live in the past.

When everything was in place, I sat in front of the bay

window in my sitting room and leaned back in Grandma's rocking chair. The seniors, including Miss Simone, had gone to Perkins' Café for a fried-chicken fund-raiser. Benjamin was working at the *Gazette* on a last-minute article. I missed him, but it was nice to have an evening to myself.

I must have dozed off, because the next thing I knew, moonlight streamed through the window. I glanced at my watch. Nine o'clock already? I stretched and looked around. The lodge was very quiet. I didn't know if I wanted to read or head downstairs and wait for the seniors. I leaned back in the rocker, relaxation flowing through my body.

Suddenly, thoughts of Trent invaded my peaceful moment, specifically the incident with the photograph. Was he lying about not being married? Irritated, I tried to shove the thoughts aside. It made no difference to me whether or not he had a wife and a dozen children. I'd already dealt with my unwanted feelings for the man, and I wasn't going to allow the enemy of my soul to pound me with condemnation. But was it really fair to Ben to continue our engagement if I could feel this attracted to another man? I shoved that thought away, too. But a niggling doubt worried at my heart.

The phone rang, and I picked up the old-fashioned Victorian-style instrument beside my chair.

"Hi, sweetheart." Benjamin's voice trilled through the curved earpiece. The bubbly feeling inside me was so different from the uncomfortable trembling that Trent's voice produced in me.

"Hi. Finish your article?"

"Yeah and covered the wingding at Perkins' as well."

"Oh, did the seniors seem to be having fun?"

He laughed. "They were having a blast. Miss Jane and Miss Georgina sang a duet. You'll never guess what."

"So tell me."

"They sang 'I'm Walking the Floor Over You.' And did the whole thing with actions."

"You're kidding. That was one of Grandpa's favorite hillbilly songs, as he called them." The thought of the two elderly ladies performing it sent me into peals of laughter. "Sounds like they had a great time. Good for them."

"How about if I come over for a while." He lowered his voice. "I miss you."

I hesitated. Should I? Maybe I'd just be hurting him. If he knew. . .

I must have hesitated too long.

"It's okay. I'll bet you're tired. . ."

"If you're sure you don't mind." Tears flooded my eyes.

"Of course not, honey. You get some rest, and I'll see you tomorrow."

The loving, caring words almost undid me.

"I love you, Victoria."

"I love you, too, Benjamin," I whispered.

A commotion downstairs alerted me to the seniors' arrival.

I blotted my eyes and went downstairs.

"Victoria, you should have been there." Miss Georgina's excited voice bounced off the foyer walls.

"I hear you and Miss Jane were the stars of the night." I smiled at them.

"Oh, who told you?" Miss Jane's eyes danced. "I'll bet it was Benjamin."

"You'd be right. He said you two were great."

"We sang your grandpa's favorite song."

"Yeah, but you'd never recognize it," Martin piped up. At a glare from Miss Evalina, he threw his hands in the air. "Just kidding, just kidding."

My offer of tea or coffee was refused by all. One by one, they trudged up the stairs.

I went into my office to turn my computer off and remembered my notebook was still in the desk drawer. I took it out and went upstairs. It was time to get a fresh look at things and do some updating.

I scanned through the list and realized I hadn't noted the lunch date of Miss Simone and Jack Riley. I also needed to note the poisoning. Could Miss Simone have slipped arsenic in his drink or food? I didn't see how anyone else could have done it. He obviously came straight back to Cedar Chapel after lunch.

As soon as Phoebe gave me the okay, I planned to have a talk with her charming uncle Jack.

After making the notations, I started to lay the pen down then paused.

What about Trent? No one really knew anything about him. What if the incident with the photograph was something more sinister than an unrevealed marriage? Chewing on the end of my pen, I sat deep in thought. It was possible. His claim to be a writer could be a cover-up for another reason to hole up in Cedar Chapel.

I was doing it again. Why did I always seem to get my head in a whirl at bedtime?

Monday morning, we were in the middle of breakfast when the phone rang. Miss Jane jumped up from the table and ran to pick it up in the kitchen, so I continued to eat my eggs.

A moment later, she appeared in the door, rolling her eyes. "Sheriff wants to talk to you, and he sounds like a rooster that just missed getting his head cut off."

I frowned. Now what could the sheriff be upset with me about, this time? I flung my napkin on the table and went to answer the phone.

"Victoria, I need to see all the seniors who knew Robert Brown in my office. Right away."

"Uh, okay. What for?"

"Never mind what for! Just tell them to get down here."

"Please?" It wouldn't hurt him to say that little word.

I heard Bob Turner's loud breath as he released it. I figured I'd better be nice before he exploded.

"We'll be there as soon as breakfast is over, Sheriff."

"We? You don't need to come. You didn't know the man."

"'Bye, Sheriff." I hung the phone up and returned to the dining room, where varying expressions of curiosity zeroed in on me.

"The sheriff wants to see everyone who knew Robert Brown. I said we'd come down after breakfast."

Miss Georgina gasped. "Oh dear."

"What?" I asked. "Do you know what he could want to talk to you about?"

She turned toward Miss Jane, an unreadable expression on her face. "Do you think he heard us talking? At the fund-raiser?"

"Probably."

"What were you talking about?" I asked.

Miss Jane took a sip of orange juice. She folded her napkin and laid it on the table then cleared her throat.

"Miss Jane?"

"Well. . .we were talking about Aggie thinking the murder victim was her dead husband. He may have heard us." She stood. "I'm going to change, if we're going downtown."

"Me, too." Miss Georgina got up and hurried after her.

I groaned. Just what we needed. The sheriff following a rabbit trail.

A half hour later, everyone, with the exception of Miss Simone, who'd never met Miss Aggie's husband, tromped into the sheriff's department. Frank had never met him either, but he insisted on going along with Miss Evalina. Deputy Lewis gave us a pitying look and, without a word, motioned for us to follow him back to the sheriff's office.

Sheriff Turner stood in the middle of the room, glaring. "So. Miz Brown thinks the murder victim is her dead husband."

He was met with total silence. Until I cleared my throat.

"Don't say a word, Victoria Storm." Was he really pointing his finger at me? "I told you not to come down here."

"Bob Turner, that's enough." Miss Evalina frowned at him, and I wondered if it would work this time. "We came down here in good faith. We've done absolutely nothing wrong. You don't need to be rude."

The sheriff sighed loudly. "Miss Swayne," he said quietly, "with all due respect, what do you call withholding evidence?"

"Nonsense, we've withheld no evidence. Everyone knows Robert Brown has been dead for years."

"Yeah? Then why would she say such a thing?"

"Because she's a ninny," Martin said, "and loves to be the center of attention."

"Now there's no call for you to talk like that about Aggie," Miss Jane retorted. "She might have been a little nervous. But how do we know she's not right?"

"Okay. None of you saw the dead man. Right?" I almost laughed out loud. Did the sheriff think we'd sneaked into the morgue?

"Oh dear." Miss Georgina looked as though she'd faint. "We don't have to look at him, do we?"

Amazed, I watched a change cross the sheriff's face. Compassion? Shame?

He cleared his throat. "No, ma'am. The body is at the medical examiner's in Springfield. You don't have to view it. I'm sorry if I said anything to make you think that."

"It's all right, Bobby." She reached over and patted his cheek, and I bit my lip to keep from grinning, as his face flamed.

Once again, he cleared his throat. "Yes, well. . ."

"So why did you want them to come down here?"

I was surprised when he didn't bite my head off for daring to speak.

"As a matter of fact, the department photographer took a head shot of him." He reached over and lifted a photo from the desk. "I'd like for those of you who knew him to take a look at this."

One by one, the seniors reluctantly took the photo, each one examining it, some closely, some quickly passing it on.

"Well?" The sheriff held the picture and looked at the seniors. "Is it him or not?"

"I don't think so," Martin said, "but I can't be sure."

"Neither can I," said Miss Georgina, shaking her head.

"Frank?" The sheriff raised his eyebrows.

"Never met the man. I was living in Kansas City back then."

"You never came back, even for a visit?" The sheriff squinted his eyes at Frank.

"Well, of course, I came to visit family. But I didn't meet Robert Brown, and if I ran across him on the street, I didn't know it was him."

The sheriff grunted and turned to Miss Evalina and Miss Jane.

Miss Evalina shrugged. "I'm sorry. I can't say. After all, he was a young man when I knew him."

Miss Jane nodded. "I can't say, either. He just looks like an old man to me."

The sheriff looked disappointed. "How about identifying marks? Can anyone think of anything?"

Again, negative head shakes.

"Okay, you can all go home. Thanks for coming down."

We filed out of the courthouse and loaded ourselves into the van.

"Well, the guy must not have had a criminal record," said Martin, "or else they'd have ID'd him by his fingerprints."

"Yeah, military's out, too," Frank mused.

When we got back to the lodge, the ladies got into Miss Jane's Caddy and the two men climbed into Frank's truck. I waved and went inside.

I put on a fresh pot of coffee then checked my answering machine and found a few messages. Mostly salespeople.

Then, "Hello, my name is Helen Banks. Please call me back at the following number." The phone number seemed to be an international number. I dialed an operator who told me the country code was Germany. I gasped. As in Jack Riley's Germany? *Oh, stop it, Victoria. He's not the only person in the world who lives in Germany.*

I slammed the sitting room phone down in frustration. Helen Banks had either changed her mind about talking to me, or it wasn't important enough to hang around for my return call. I'd been trying to reach her all morning, to no avail. There wasn't even a recording or a way to leave a message.

Walking over to the window, I sat in the nearby rocking chair. I'd pretty much wasted the day so far, having been unable to concentrate on anything except the elusive Helen Banks. Who could she be, and what could she want to talk to me about?

Was her place of residence really a coincidence? Or could she have something to do with Jack Riley?

Well, phooey. I had things to do. With resolution, I left the room, not even glancing at the phone as I walked out. When I got downstairs, the first thing I did was snatch up the hall phone and dial. Still no answer.

I headed for the front porch and sat on the swing. At least there was no phone out here. Hmm. Maybe I should have gotten that cell phone I'd been promising myself.

I was happy to see Benjamin's truck pull up and park at the curb.

"Hi, honey." He grinned as he stepped up on the porch.

I turned my face up as he leaned in to kiss me.

"I tried to call, but your line was busy. I thought you might like to go to lunch."

"Yeah. I guess." Realizing I probably didn't sound very eager to be with him, I smiled and squeezed his hand. "If you'll wait for me to change."

"You're fine. We can just grab something at Perkins' Café or the Mocha Java."

"Okay, give me a minute." I rushed up the stairs and ran a brush over my hair then frowned at my reflection in the mirror. I'd forgotten my appointment with Millie. I sighed. Oh well. Shrugging, I ran down the stairs to Miss Simone's door and knocked.

When she said to come in, I opened the door. "Miss Simone, I'm going to lunch with Benjamin. Mabel made minestrone for us to heat up for lunch today. Would you like me to bring you a tray before I leave?"

"No, I'm not hungry. I may have a sandwich later."

"Okay, soup'll keep. Can I bring you something back from the café?"

"No, thank you. I'm going to write some letters, then perhaps I'll go out."

I hurried downstairs, and Benjamin and I headed out to the truck.

Perkins' was crowded, but we managed to find an empty booth.

Hannah's teenage niece, Amber, rushed over and cleaned the table. "Be right back with your water," she said, slinging two menus down in front of us.

Benjamin stared after her. "Was that Amber?"

"Yep. Doesn't seem possible, does it?"

"Seems like yesterday she was sitting in the back booth combing her doll's hair." He craned his neck to follow her movements. "I don't think she recognized me."

I laughed. "She was only six when they moved away."

"A shame about the divorce."

"Yeah, I know. Her mother is working for an attorney in Branson, and they're staying with Hannah until they get on their feet."

Amber brought two tall, frosted glasses of ice water. "Are you ready to order?"

We ordered sandwiches and iced tea and handed her the menus.

"Shouldn't she be in school?" Benjamin watched the girl walk away.

"She is. She's in college."

"Oh. Hey, I saw you and the gang going into the courthouse earlier."

Ah. That's why he'd been trying to call and why he invited me to lunch today.

"Umm-hmm."

"Umm-hmm?"

I laughed. "Sheriff Turner overheard a couple of the ladies talking about Miss Aggie's suspicions about the dead man."

"Uh-oh."

"Yeah, he showed them a photo, but they couldn't tell

if it was Robert Brown or not."

He smiled at Amber as she set our tea on the table. "Thanks."

"Miss Aggie has quite an imagination," he said. "She's also very melodramatic."

"I know. But there must have been some reason for her to think that."

"Maybe."

"Something else happened today." I stirred sugar into my tea and told him about the phone call from Germany.

"And you think she has connections to our Jack Riley?"

"I don't know. Not really."

"So you don't think she has connections to him, but you do think it's suspicious that they're both from Germany?"

I frowned at his grinning face. "I didn't say that. I'm not sure what I think."

"Oh well. If it's important, she'll probably call back."

"I'm confused."

"I know you are, sweetheart, but that's okay. I love you anyway."

⟡

I waved good-bye to Benjamin in front of the lodge.

"Yoo-hoo! Victoria!" Mrs. Miller hurried down the sidewalk. She stopped beside me and stood trying to catch her breath.

"Are you all right?"

"Yes, yes," she gasped, holding her side. "I shouldn't have rushed like that. But I have something to tell you."

I waited while her breathing slowed.

"Okay. I'm fine." She exhaled slowly.

"You had me worried there for a minute. What did you want to tell me?"

"I asked Gerald about Jack Riley, like I said I would." She eyed me closely.

"Oh? Did your husband know Mr. Riley?"

"He sure did. Said he left here when he was a young man."

"I see. Well, I'd better get inside, Mrs. Miller. It was nice talking to you."

"Oh, of course, dear. I only wondered if you knew he was an old friend of Jenny Simon's."

"As a matter of fact, he told me that himself." There. That should burst her bubble.

"Did he tell you he was very much in love with her?"

I couldn't hide my surprise, and her expression brightened with satisfaction.

"Gerald said Jack Riley would have just about killed for Jenny Simon."

I managed a polite escape and went inside. Before I had time to digest the new information, Mabel met me at the door. "I think Miss Simone's come down with something. She's been in her room since breakfast."

"I'll go up and check on her."

"And Miz Brown called. She sounded madder than a wet hen."

Oh no. What now? I dialed Simon Pennington's Jefferson City phone number. Miss Aggie answered on the second ring.

"Hi, Miss Aggie. You called?"

"What's going on there? Bob Turner called and ordered me back home." Mabel was right. Miss Aggie was very angry.

I told her about the trip to the sheriff's office.

"So what does he want from me?"

"I'm not sure, Miss Aggie. I guess he'll tell you when he sees you." If I told her he wanted her to look at a picture and see if it was her husband, she'd probably plant herself firmly in Jefferson City, no matter what the sheriff said.

"I'll be home in the morning. Make sure my room is aired out."

"Of course, Miss Aggie. I'll see to it. It'll be nice to have you home. We've missed you."

"All right then. I'll see you when I get there."

She hung up, and I sank into the chair by the hall phone, feeling worn out. There was so much going on that my head was spinning. Or was I blowing everything out of proportion? I needed a vacation.

I tried Helen Banks's number again. Still no answer. Still no recording. Still no way to leave a message. What was it with that woman?

Frank and Martin walked in, followed by the ladies. They all waved and headed to the rec room.

"Would you like to join us in a game of canasta, Victoria?" Miss Jane called back over her shoulder.

"No thanks, I've got things to do. Miss Aggie's coming home tomorrow."

Miss Jane's face lit up. "I'm so glad." She hurried after the others.

"Mabel, I'm going up to check on Miss Simone, then I'll touch up Miss Aggie's room," I said, walking into the kitchen. "She'll be home in the morning."

"Anything special I need to know?"

"Not really. She's not picky about food. She's partial to fried chicken, so maybe we should have that tomorrow night to welcome her home. And strawberry shortcake for dessert. Sorry to switch the menu on you."

"No problem. Fried chicken's my specialty." She gave a final shake to the salad dressing she was mixing.

"Thanks, you're a blessing."

I tapped on Miss Simone's door, and when I got no reply, I opened it and peeked in. She was sound asleep. I walked over softly and listened to her breathing. It was even, and she didn't appear flushed, so I left and closed the door. She probably just didn't want to be disturbed.

Miss Aggie's room was nearly spotless but smelled like stale Chanel No. 5. I opened the window then went to the hall closet and took out a dust cloth and polish. A quick wipe over the furniture and the room was in top shape. I left the window open. I'd let it air for a while and then close it before opening the air-conditioning vent.

Finally, I climbed the third-floor stairs to my room. I sank into my recliner and closed my eyes. My mind drifted to the conversation with Mrs. Miller. Should I put any stock in what she'd told me? She was such a gossip. She may have it all wrong. And even if Mr. Riley had been in love with Miss Simone, so what? People fell in love when they were young. Usually, if nothing came of it, they got over it. But. . .what if he hadn't gotten over it? Maybe Miss Simone did know the murdered man. He could have followed her here. Would Jack Riley have killed him in a jealous rage?

I took my notebook out and added the new information with a question mark. Funny though, when I looked over the list, I realized almost everything in it went back in some way to Miss Simone.

18

Sheriff Turner looked at Miss Aggie. "Are you sure?"

"Of course I'm sure. It's not him. Don't you think I'd know my own husband?"

"Yes, but he was a fairly young man when he died, wasn't he?"

For the first time since looking at the photo, uncertainty shadowed Miss Aggie's eyes.

I stepped closer to her, and the other ladies, as one, seemed to press in, surrounding, protecting their friend.

The sheriff stepped back in surprise and then raked his fingers through his hair.

"All right, Miz Brown, but I do have one more question."

"Very well, Bob. What is it?" Miss Aggie sounded tired, and I noticed she wasn't looking as spunky today as usual.

"Did Robert have any scars or other identifying marks? A birthmark, maybe?"

She furrowed her brow and bit her lip as she thought. "No, I can't think of anything. Oh. Wait. Yes. There was something."

The sheriff's face came alive, his eyes alert and eager. "What was it, Miz Brown?"

"He had a tattoo."

"I don't remember a tattoo, Aggie," Miss Jane said, with a puzzled look.

Miss Aggie blushed, and I laughed inwardly, suspecting what was coming.

"You wouldn't have known, Jane, because it wasn't visible to just anyone." She glanced at me. "Could I whisper to you, Victoria? Then you can tell the sheriff."

"Of course, Miss Aggie."

"Now wait just a minute, Miz Brown," the sheriff said. "If you have information, you need to tell me directly. And I mean right now."

Miss Aggie huffed and glared at the sheriff. "Fine," she snapped.

She glanced around. "I hope this isn't too embarrassing for anyone. If it is, it's Bob's fault."

Tightening her lips, she looked straight at the sheriff. "Robert Brown had a hootchy-kootchy dancer tattooed on his backside." She paused then continued with flair, "She wiggled when he walked."

Gasps emanated from Miss Jane and Miss Georgina. Miss Evalina closed her eyes and looked pained.

I choked back laughter as Bob Turner's face paled then flamed red. Quickly, he got control, and disappointment replaced his embarrassment. Apparently, a tattoo on the backside wasn't what he had been expecting.

"Okay, Miss Aggie," he said. "We can rule out Robert Brown as the victim. I expect your husband is resting in the grave where you buried him."

Miss Aggie's entire countenance changed as relief washed over her face. Apparently, she'd been more worried than I'd realized.

"Well then." Her voice had returned to its usual strength and confidence, with a touch of arrogance. "Let's get out of here."

Miss Jane threw a glance at the sheriff that dared him to stop us, and we all trooped out.

"I'd say this calls for a celebration," I said.

"Good idea, Victoria," Miss Aggie said. "I was too nervous to eat lunch. Could we get something?"

"Of course. What sounds good?"

"Banana splits." Her eyes danced as we got in the van. She seemed truly cheerful for the first time since the body showed up at Pennington House.

We headed for the Dairy Joy on the edge of town. It was a favorite teen hangout, but since school was in session, we pretty much had the place to ourselves.

We dug into our banana splits. What a relief to sit with friends and relax. Now that Miss Aggie's fear turned out to be unfounded, a load seemed to lift off all of us.

"Before we return to the lodge, I'd like to go by Pennington House." Miss Aggie's eyes sparkled as she glanced around at us. "But maybe while we're here, you could tell me all about the cave and tunnel you found beneath my house."

Oh, Miss Aggie. So much for relaxing. The whole mystery came tumbling back down on my head.

Between Miss Jane and Miss Georgina, with occasional input from Miss Evalina and me, we managed to tell the story fairly accurately. Although Miss Jane did attempt some embellishment.

A little nervous, I awaited Miss Aggie's reaction.

"Wonderful. I couldn't have thought up a story that would have been better for business. We'll advertise about pirate's treasure and give tours."

"Uh, Miss Aggie, I thought the new hotel and restaurant were supposed to be the epitome of refinement. Sort of like the excusive establishments in Europe."

"Well, they are. What's wrong with pirate treasure?

Ghost stories never hurt business in England and Ireland. And the converted plantation houses down south nearly all have ghosts." She frowned at me. "I know all about these things. I've done a lot of research."

I lifted my hands in surrender and apologized. She was right. I knew absolutely nothing about these things. I just hoped she and Corky didn't cross horns over the subject.

Corky and his crew were busy at work when we arrived at Pennington House. Corky waved to us and spoke to the man he was consulting with. The man nodded, and Corky headed in our direction.

"Aunt Aggie. It's a good thing you're back. We can barely run things without you here."

"Umm-hmm. You'd better say that, young man." Aggie grinned and tolerated the kiss Corky planted on her cheek.

"What do you want to see first?"

"Did you get the old kitchen walled up like I told you to?"

"Yes, ma'am. Come see."

We followed him through the kitchen and down the hall to the utility room, which used to be the kitchen when the house was first built.

The secret doorway and the tunnel were now hidden behind a smooth, painted wall lined with shelves. Commercial washers and dryers lined one wall. Miss Aggie opened a door and revealed an enormous hot-water heater.

She nodded in satisfaction and closed the door. "We never had enough hot water at Pennington."

We went back through the house and out onto the porch.

"Are you ready to go to the lodge now, Miss Aggie?"

She glanced around then looked at me. "I'd like to see the cave."

Before I could protest, she'd turned and gone back into the house. The rest of us trailed after her as she went through the library, down the carpeted tunnel, and into the secret room.

Miss Aggie stood and looked around the room. "This is as far as I've gone. When the workers told me about the tunnel they'd found with the body, I knew it must lead to this room, the same as the one leading from the library. But I had no idea there was another tunnel branching off or that there was a cave."

Miss Jane walked over to the fireplace and reached in. It swung back, and the door was revealed. Miss Aggie opened it and stepped into the tunnel.

Surprised, I watched her reach into her handbag and take out a flashlight. Apparently, the lady had planned ahead.

"Perhaps you should go first, Victoria. I have no idea where I'm going." She stood aside, and I walked past her.

"I'd like to see the tracks Ben uncovered, as well as the cave," she said. Her voice echoed down the tunnel.

I led the way, with the others following. This time, the trek down the tunnel didn't seem nearly as suspenseful and not at all frightening. Miss Aggie examined the tracks carefully.

When we arrived at the intersection, we turned into the other tunnel. We were all getting tired by the time we reached the cave.

Miss Aggie stood in the center of the huge cavern. She walked over to the wall and followed it around, feeling as she went. She examined the wood pallets then followed the uncovered track to the outside entrance. She stepped through, and the rest of us followed.

Miss Aggie turned and looked at the opening through which we'd exited the cave.

"How in the world did we miss this, Jane?"

Miss Jane shook her head. "I think there must have been something else hiding the opening. I've no idea what. But surely we'd have seen this."

Miss Aggie pushed through the tree branches and bushes, and suddenly, we stood staring at the river.

"I simply don't understand. We used to swim in this river." She ran her hand over her eyes.

"Yes, but, Aggie," Miss Georgina piped up, "we didn't swim in this area. We swam farther upriver. Don't you remember? Your father forbade us to swim or play down this way."

"That's right. I do remember. He told us there were rattlesnakes here and currents in this part of the river. He said we could get pulled under." She gave a rueful laugh. "I'm surprised the boys fell for that."

"They may not have. Martin said all the smuggling or whatever it was probably happened at night."

"But wouldn't we have seen or heard something? Remember all the lawn parties we used to have? Of course the river doesn't run that close to the house."

"No," Miss Jane agreed. "I think we may be more than a mile from the house at this point. It seemed like a longer walk than that through the tunnel." She rubbed at her back.

"Speaking of the tunnel, we have quite a return walk, ladies." I hated to interrupt their walk down memory lane, but we needed to head back. Personally, I hoped I'd be as active as they were when I was their age. "Do you think I could drive the van down here?"

"I wouldn't try it. You don't have four-wheel drive, do you?"

"No, but Corky's truck does. Let me come back for you."

"I'm not waiting," Miss Jane said.

The other two agreed, so I gave up, and we started back through the tunnel together.

I trudged up the stairs with a pail of hot water for Miss Aggie's foot massager. The other ladies who'd taken part in our little excursion were resting in front of the television. Except one. I had a hunch Miss Jane, who had gone to her room early, was lying in bed with a heating pad on her back. I'd noticed her rubbing it as she limped upstairs.

I made a mental note to be more careful with the seniors. I was so used to them being active that I sometimes forgot their age.

The house seemed more normal now that Miss Aggie was ensconced in her room. I knew I'd miss her when Pennington House was completed and she moved out there.

As I passed the back parlor on my way to the recreation room, a thin stream of light from beneath the door drew my attention. Figuring someone had left it on, I opened the door then drew back. Too late. They'd spotted me.

"It's quite all right, Victoria. We've been planning to speak to you anyway." Miss Evalina motioned to me from the sofa where she sat beside Frank. "Come in, please."

Butterflies jumped in my stomach. Had they set a date? I sat on one of the overstuffed armchairs across from the sofa.

"I still can't believe she said yes after all this time." Frank's face was red with excitement, and joy exploded from his voice. "We were childhood sweethearts. Did I ever tell you that? And I never stopped loving her."

A quiet radiance rested on Miss Evalina's face as she sent him a look of fond amusement.

"I'm so happy for you both," I said, meaning it from the bottom of my heart. "So, have you set a date?"

"Tomorrow," Frank said, beaming at his intended.

"Frank!" Miss Evalina laughed. "Stop that."

He chortled. "I suggested tomorrow, but Eva wants to wait a few weeks until this murder business is cleared up."

"That's right," she said. "I want no shadow hanging over our celebration. We'd like to have a small ceremony here at the lodge, if that is acceptable to you, Victoria."

"Of course it is, Miss Evalina. It would be an honor."

"We'll announce the date as soon as we've decided. We want to tell Frank Junior and Sylvia first." A shadow of doubt passed over her face.

Frank squeezed her hand. "Now, sweetheart, the kids will be happy. Don't you worry."

The confidence in his voice apparently reassured her, because she smiled. "Of course they will. I know they love me, almost as much as I love them."

Frank's son and daughter-in-law, who lived in Branson, were lovely people, and I had no doubt they were thrilled at Frank's happiness.

I congratulated them both and made a hasty exit, leaving them to their plans.

Ten minutes later, a glass of iced tea in hand, I leaned back in the porch swing and sighed with relief. What a day! At least it had a nice ending, with Miss Evalina and Frank's news. Their friends would be so happy for them.

I looked up as the screen door creaked open and Miss Aggie stepped outside.

"Why, Miss Aggie. I thought you'd be sound asleep by now."

She sighed and sat beside me. "Couldn't sleep. I need to get some things out into the open. Maybe it'll help solve this crime, maybe not."

"All right, then. I'm all ears."

"I want to tell the others, too. Should have confided in them years ago, I guess."

"I think Miss Jane is asleep."

"Yes, I stopped by her room, and she was sleeping like a log. And Georgina was going up as I was coming down."

"What would you like to do then?"

"Wait until morning, I suppose."

"Are you sure?"

"Yes, it's waited this long. It'll wait until morning." She leaned back and sighed. "Why don't you call Benjamin and ask him to come over? I'll call Corky."

"Okay. Why don't we invite them for breakfast, and we can gather in the parlor afterward?"

"That'll work." She sighed. "Victoria, it's very difficult for me to discuss my family."

"I understand." And I did.

"Tomorrow, then." She stood, and I watched as she went back inside the house.

Until a few months ago, few Cedar Chapel residents

had remembered, if they'd ever known, that Miss Aggie Brown was a member of the wealthy Pennington family. She'd lived quietly and frugally for many years in a small house then, for the last few years, here at the lodge while Pennington House stood deserted. An abandoned castle on top of a hill.

I'd been shocked last year when the seniors had informed me that their friend, missing at the time, was the Pennington heiress. I'd known her all my life. But her secret had been well kept by all her lifelong friends, including my grandparents.

Of course, that all changed when Corky had moved to Cedar Chapel and the two of them had decided to turn Pennington House into a luxury hotel. Before long, Miss Aggie had morphed back into heiress mode. She'd traded in her old car for a brand-new Lexus, went shopping for new clothes, and changed her name back to the hyphenated Pennington-Brown. The town of Cedar Chapel looked on in amazement. Except for her friends and, of course her banker, who'd known all along. One thing she didn't change was her perfume. She'd never given up her Chanel No. 5.

19

The little mantle clock ticked off the minutes as we sat expectantly, waiting for Miss Aggie to begin. Benjamin, with a reporter's typical patience, sat calmly, antenna up, ready to sift through what he would hear and mentally record the pertinent facts. I could almost hear the wheels turning in his mind as he waited. Miss Simone, to my relief, was in her suite.

Corky rubbed the toe of one shoe against the heel of another and squirmed, giving action to what I was feeling.

Miss Aggie looked around the group and bit her lip.

"I hope you haven't built things up in your mind so that you think I have something life shattering to say."

"Of course not." I hoped I was speaking for everyone else. I wasn't speaking for myself. I'd been building the possibilities up in my mind all night.

She set her coffee cup on the table by her chair and licked her upper lip.

"I've known about the emeralds since I was a girl. But I had no idea then, nor do I now, where they came from. I found out about them quite by accident." Her lips trembled, and she pressed them together for a moment. "I had just turned eighteen. It was during the war years. I remember there was a dance in Caffee Springs I wanted to attend. I walked into the library to get permission from my father. He was leaning against a bookcase and was looking down at something in his hands. When I realized what he held, I gasped, and he looked up, startled.

"I asked him if the emeralds were a present for mother, but he mumbled something about a family heirloom that he'd removed from the safe for cleaning. Then, he showed them to me, telling me they were worth a fortune. I'm sure they were. There were several pieces. A choker-type necklace. A large heart-shaped stone on a gold chain, two bracelets, and a set of earrings. I thought at the time it was strange I'd never heard about them before.

"He gave me permission to go to the dance, and I forgot all about the emeralds. After all, he'd just presented me with the diamond pendant and earrings a few weeks earlier, and my mother had said I could wear them to the dance."

"So you never saw the emeralds again?" I had to ask.

"Oh yes. I saw them. After my parents passed away, I was surprised to find them in my father's safe. I have no idea why he didn't keep them in a vault at the bank. I intended to do just that, but of course, my inheritance was put on hold, and I had no access to anything except an allowance and my personal belongings until the ruling was finally overturned."

I still thought that had been unjust of her father. But the sad fact was that she had married a gold digger just as her father had feared might happen, and if Robert Brown hadn't been killed, he would have probably squandered her entire inheritance.

"When I realized the emeralds had disappeared, I assumed Robert had gambled them away, but now, with the story Corky told me, I'm not so sure. Of course, the story was mixed up, but I'm rather suspicious that Forrest may have been involved somehow. I'll probably never know."

She looked around from one to the other. "And now, you know the story of the emeralds. I realize, in light of the discoveries at Pennington House, the jewels might not be family heirlooms. I'm not even sure now if my diamonds are legitimately mine."

Suddenly, her eyes filled, and tears fell silently from her eyes. Angrily, she wiped them away.

"No, Aggie, your father bought your diamonds. I know he did." Miss Jane stood and went to her friend. She leaned over and put her arm around Miss Aggie's shoulders. "Besides, he put your diamonds in the bank vault, didn't he?"

Miss Aggie's eyes brightened. "Yes, you're right, Jane. He kept them at the bank except for when I wanted to wear them. So they couldn't have been. . ."

"Well, of course, they couldn't have been," Miss Evalina said, sharply. "Don't be a goose, Aggie. Your father wouldn't have given you stolen jewelry."

A hush fell on the room. The word had been spoken.

Miss Aggie inhaled deeply and let her breath out in a *whoosh*. "Thank you, Eva."

"In fact," I said, "we don't know for sure if anything was stolen. And if there was something illegal going on, we don't know that Mr. Pennington was involved."

Heads from snow-white to steel gray nodded. And Miss Aggie's head of dyed black hair bobbed as well.

"What would I do without you, my friends?"

I breathed a sigh of relief. All was well for the moment, but there was one question that needed to be answered.

"Miss Aggie, what do you know about Jack Riley? And how do you think he knew about the jewels?"

"What are you suggesting, Victoria?" Corky snapped.

"Are you implying Phoebe's uncle is a crook?"

"I didn't imply any such thing, Corky Pennington." He *did* have it bad.

A penitent look crossed his face. "Sorry. Guess I misunderstood."

Benjamin sat up straight, and I'd have known that alert expression anywhere. He wanted to hear what Miss Aggie said about Mr. Riley as much as I did.

She frowned. "Jack was older than our crowd, and he moved away, of course. I'm not even sure I remember him."

I glanced toward the door, to make sure Miss Simone was nowhere in sight. "Is it true that he was in love with Miss Simone?"

"Well, how should I know? What does that have to do with anything?" Ah, Miss Aggie was back to her old self again.

I hastened to change the subject. "So, he wanted to see your diamonds?"

"Yes, as well as other family heirlooms, and when I refused, he asked me about the emeralds."

"But how did he know about the emeralds?"

"I really don't know. Robert may have said something, but Jack had left town by then." She appeared confused.

"Never mind, Miss Aggie. I don't suppose it's important."

"But maybe it is," she protested. "How *would* he know about them? No one outside the family knew. At least, I don't think they did."

Corky got up. "I need to go to Pennington House. The workers will be waiting for me. Aunt Aggie, are you coming with me?" He darted one of those looks at me as he held his hand out to her. I wasn't sure who he was most protective of, Phoebe or Miss Aggie.

Miss Aggie rose and said good-bye and left with her nephew. Shortly afterward, the rest of the gang left for the center, leaving Benjamin and me sitting in the parlor alone.

"So?" I asked with a grin. If I'd had doubts about Jack Riley being of interest, those doubts were gone. The fact that he knew about the emeralds spoke volumes. I wasn't sure just what. But volumes nevertheless.

"He knows about the emeralds, and Miss Aggie has no idea how he knows," Benjamin said.

"Yeah. So? What do you think?"

"I think, so what? He could have heard about them from anyone. Rumors fly when money is involved. And in his line of business, it's natural he'd be interested."

I looked at him. "You really disappoint me sometimes, Benjamin." I stood and headed for the door.

"Victoria, wait."

I turned, surprised at the seriousness of his voice.

He walked over to me and cupped my chin with his hand. "Honey, I haven't been idle. And I haven't been ignoring you. I'm investigating every concern you have. Jack Riley and Jeannette Simone, as well as the possible smuggling at Pennington in the past."

"Then why—?"

"I don't want you involved, sweetheart. If there is current criminal activity going on, things could get dangerous. Especially if the murder is connected in some way and isn't just a random crime."

I snuggled closer to him. "I know you worry about me, and I'll be careful. Promise me you will, too."

"I promise." He leaned down and kissed me. "I need to get to the office. I'll call you later."

I walked him to the door and watched as he drove off. My Benjamin. I should have known he wouldn't let me down.

———

I paced up and down the hallway outside Miss Simone's room. Should I? Or not? It seemed too good to be true that she'd left right after lunch, announcing she wouldn't be here for dinner. It was an almost irresistible opportunity to check out her suite and see if I could find anything linking her to the crime.

An uncomfortable feeling of déjà vu washed over me. I'd had this same inner struggle over checking out Miss Aggie's room when she was missing. On the one hand, I had hated to invade her privacy, but on the other, there was a lot at stake. What was the right thing to do?

The memory of Miss Aggie in the hands of the bank robbers last year assured me I'd done the right thing then. But was this anywhere near the same thing?

I continued to pace. The memory of Miss Simone's ashen face and trembling hands when she'd been on the phone made me catch my breath. Something was wrong. She could be in danger. Or, if she herself was involved, my friends could be in danger.

Lifting my chin with resolution, I opened her door and walked in. Darkness enveloped the room. Not a thread of light made it through the lowered blinds and heavy drapes that hung on the window. I switched on the overhead light and did a quick scan of the sitting room from where I stood.

Suddenly, a wave of guilt washed over me. I turned

off the light and rushed out into the hall, stopping just in time to keep from running over Miss Jane.

"I had a feeling we'd find you here. But why are you leaving?" Miss Jane's forehead wrinkled with confusion.

"It's illegal and immoral to go through Miss Simone's room."

"It's not illegal," Miss Jane reasoned. "This is your house, and Jenny's door is unlocked. Besides, you come in to clean her room every day."

"That's not the same." Or was it? "How did you know I'd be here?"

"Mabel said you were upstairs, so when we couldn't find you anywhere else, we thought you must be searching Jenny's room." Miss Georgina appeared a little scandalized, ironic after the part she'd played in going through Miss Aggie's room.

"I'm surprised you didn't do this sooner," Miss Jane said with a nod of her head. "But we have to be careful."

"We?"

"Of course," said Miss Jane. "It'll be quicker. And we need to be quick. Martin's watching for Jenny."

"Thanks, ladies. But I don't think this is a good idea."

Miss Georgina nodded. "It wouldn't surprise me if Jenny sued you if she caught you going through her things."

My stomach flipped, and a wave of nausea went through me. That would be just great. I could see the headlines now. Victoria Storm Arrested for Breaking and Entering. Swallowing, I shoved the thought aside.

"Well, I'm going in there, and I'm not coming out until I've searched the whole room." Miss Jane glared at us, determination shooting from both eyes.

Okay, I couldn't let her do this alone. If we both got caught, I could take the blame. I stepped in behind Miss Jane and felt Miss Georgina's breath on my neck as she followed.

We did a quick search of the sitting room, which revealed nothing, then went into Miss Simone's bedroom.

"This is more like it," Miss Jane said

I had to agree. The century-old highboy, the dresser with a dozen drawers. Secrets could easily be hidden here.

Miss Jane and I headed for the highboy, while Miss Georgina scurried over to the closet.

Miss Simone's dresser was neat, her things precisely organized. The top drawer held cosmetics and similar items. Stacks of undergarments and nightgowns filled the others.

Frustrated, I'd just about decided we were on the wrong track.

"Victoria. Jane. Look." Miss Georgina held a stack of picture albums in her arms.

We divided them up between us.

"Anything you might think is suspicious. Even the smallest suspicion. Okay?"

Affirmative murmurs answered me, and I opened one of the albums. It turned out to be filled with memorabilia from Miss Simone's acting years. Interesting but nothing jumped out at me.

The next one was more personal. Apparently, family pictures. I turned a page, and my eyes fell on the first inkling of a clue I'd seen so far. The photo was obviously a younger Miss Simone and a younger Jack Riley. They stood in front of a palm tree. The little girl in Jack Riley's arms couldn't have been more than two. Could this be the baby of the rumors? I looked more closely. All three were laughing. His arm was around Miss Simone, and her hand rested on the child's back.

"I've found something," I said, trying to contain my excitement.

Miss Jane and Miss Georgina hurried over and exclaimed at the discovery.

We looked at the other photos on the two open pages. All of the same three people. Excitement swelled inside me. Looked like a family to me.

The album contained photos from every stage of the child's life up to her high school graduation. I closed it and eagerly reached for another, while the ladies went back to the other albums.

I opened the cover. The first page was a picture of the girl's wedding, and then came photos of a little girl in varying stages of growth. I turned another page. This time, a photo of a teenage boy looked very familiar, but I wasn't sure. Surprise and excitement began to grow in me. I turned another page.

"Jackpot!" I sat back with a smile of satisfaction while Miss Georgina and Miss Jane leaned over the album.

Miss Georgina gasped as she looked at the young man standing with Miss Simone.

"That's Trent Stewart with Jenny," I announced.

Miss Jane looked at me in astonishment. "You mean the writer fellow who moved to town?"

"I never even suspected," Miss Georgina said, her eyes wide.

"Me, either," I said. "But the fact they've kept their relationship, whatever it is, a secret doesn't bode well."

"I'll bet he's Jenny's grandson." Miss Jane's eyes sparkled with excitement.

Miss Georgina's head bobbed up and down. "I was going to say the same thing."

Could they be right? I couldn't deny the thought had crossed my mind as well.

"Well, regardless of how they know each other, I need to make copies of these photos." I reached for the album, but Miss Jane grabbed my hand.

"No. Victoria, they're old. They might be stuck to the glue. You don't want to tear the photo."

She was right, of course. "I'll take the album down and scan the pages."

"Well, hurry. Jenny might decide to come home early or something."

"I don't think so. She said she wouldn't be here for dinner."

The three of us hurried downstairs, where Martin still kept watch by the front door.

"Find anything?" he asked, his face a picture of curiosity.

"Yes, we'll tell you in a minute," I said, as I hurried to my office.

I managed to get a fairly good copy scanned and printed, and we hurried back upstairs and deposited the albums safely in their spot on the closet shelf.

Ten minutes later, we fell onto sofas and chairs in the sitting room.

"This calls for a few minutes of relaxation," Miss Jane said, panting. "I could sure use a hot cup of tea."

"My thoughts exactly," I said, jumping up. "I'll get it."

Mabel gave me a funny look as I stepped into the kitchen. "What have you people been up to? I heard you rushing through the house, and Miss Georgina was breathing so loud I could hear her in here."

I thought fast. Now what could I say that wouldn't be an out-and-out lie but not reveal anything?

"Just doing a little investigating. That's all. You know how excited Miss Georgina gets over every little thing." Oh my, had I really said that?

Mabel eyed me. "Uh-huh. Go on in the parlor. I'll bring the tea."

"Thanks, Mabel."

As I rejoined the others, a thought came to me. That framed picture that Trent had knocked over could have been one of Miss Simone. And if he felt he needed to hide it, something was definitely going on that shouldn't be. Should I confront him? Then a chill went through me. Had I spent a stormy morning in a lonely cabin with a murderer?

20

A few minutes later, true to her word, Mabel pushed the tea cart through the door of the front parlor. We thanked her, and she left the room. I didn't figure there was any need to pull her into the problem. Besides, as much as I liked and admired Mabel, I hadn't really known her that long.

Frank and Miss Evalina appeared in the doorway, took one look at our flushed faces, and started pummeling us with questions, which Miss Jane and Miss Georgina both rushed to answer.

"We were searching. . ."

"We found these. . ."

They both stopped.

"Why don't we wait until we have our tea, and then we can explain," I suggested.

I poured the tea and handed cups to everyone then sat back gratefully against the soft cushions. I'd wanted Benjamin to be here, but when I'd tried to call and got his recording, I'd left a message that I needed to see him.

"Victoria, why don't you tell them?" Miss Jane said.

"All right." I'd just have to fill Benjamin in later. "Anyway, there's something you don't know about that, that I'd better let you in on first."

I told them about the day of the storm and my visit to Trent Stewart's cabin.

"Victoria Storm, do you mean to tell us you went into a house alone with a man you hardly know?" Miss Evalina's expression was a mixture of worry, disappointment, and disapproval.

"I know it was a foolish thing to do. I could have dropped him off and pulled to the side of the road until the storm was over."

Quickly, I went on to share the information about the strange phone call from the elusive Helen Banks in Germany.

"And she hasn't called back? That is rather strange." Frank frowned.

"I intend to keep trying to reach her. But now, on to the real news."

I wasn't sure how Miss Evalina and the men would react to our searching the suite, so I thought I'd better pave the way.

"I'm sure you'll recall that I've had some suspicions of Miss Simone because of some of her actions lately." I paused, and they all nodded. Miss Jane and Miss Georgina had eager looks on their faces.

"I didn't really think she killed anyone, but I thought she might possibly know something and that someone could be threatening her because of that."

"So we decided to search her room," Miss Georgina's excited voice interrupted. I'd intended to try to keep her and Miss Jane out of it, so that Miss Evalina's disapproval would only rain down on me. So much for good intentions.

"Well, did you find anything incriminating?" Miss Evalina's words delighted me, and I grinned. I never knew what to expect from this precious lady.

I picked up the folder from the cushion next to me and opened it with a flourish, presenting the copy of the photo.

Miss Evalina, Martin, and Frank leaned over and

peered at the photo. Their initial reaction seemed to be confusion. I couldn't blame them. I'd been momentarily confused when I first saw the picture, too.

"So what do you think?" I asked, looking at Miss Evalina.

She cleared her throat. "Hmm. Apparently, Jenny knows Cedar Chapel's newest resident."

Disappointed, I said, "But don't you think it's strange that she hasn't mentioned it?"

"Why would she mention it? Does she ever talk about her personal life to any of us?" Miss Evalina stood up. "I'm going to rest until dinner."

"I guess I will, too." Miss Georgina scurried after her, and they climbed the stairs together.

"Well, if that doesn't beat all." Miss Jane frowned after them.

"Eva's right," said Frank. "I don't know why you got all excited because Jenny knows Trent Stewart. How about a game of cards before dinner, Martin?"

I couldn't tell if Martin agreed with him, but he followed Frank down the hall to the rec room.

"Well, Miss Jane. It looks like it's up to you and me to investigate this matter."

"You can count me in, dear. You know you can. But please," she said, throwing me a grin, "let's stay away from tunnels."

Laughing, I headed out the door. "I promise I'll try my best to stay away from tunnels. I don't like them, either."

As I walked into the foyer, the phone rang and I answered. "Cedar Lodge."

"Hi, sweetheart. I just got your message." Relief washed over me at the sound of my guy's voice.

"Benjamin, hi. Are you busy?"

"Sort of. I'm on my way to an interview. What's up?"

"I need to talk to you about something important. But it can wait until later. How about coming to dinner?"

"Sorry, I'm tied up for dinner. I can come over afterward."

"That'll be great. I'll see you then."

"Are you sure everything is okay? I'll scrap the business dinner if you say the word."

"No, no. After dinner is fine. I'll see you then."

As I hung up the phone, Miss Jane stepped into the foyer.

"Victoria, what are your plans?" she asked.

"You know, I think we should wait until I can talk to Benjamin before we jump into anything." Wow, had I really said that?

Her eyes filled with relief. "Good, because I think I'll go rest awhile before dinner."

"Good idea. I might go upstairs and write to my parents. Or maybe I'll call. They're in London this week." Dad insisted on sending me money each month to cover long-distance calls. Mom and Dad had tried time and again to talk me into accepting an allowance from them, but I wanted to make it on my own. I figured with the Lord's help and the small income from my grandparents' estate I was doing pretty well. And in another year or so, I should be showing a small profit from the boardinghouse. But the money for phone calls was a different matter entirely. I didn't hesitate to take it, with thanks.

When I got my dad's funny recording, I left a message. It was still a couple of hours before dinner, so I showered and bundled up in my terrycloth robe. I leaned back in the recliner and closed my eyes. The ringing of the phone awakened me. Startled, I grabbed the receiver.

"Hello?"

"Hello? Is this Cedar Lodge?"

"Yes, sorry, the phone startled me. Victoria Storm speaking."

"Miss Storm, My name is Helen Banks. I'm calling from Berlin."

"Oh. Yes, Ms. Banks. I'm sorry I missed your call before. How may I help you?"

"I'll be in Cedar Chapel next week. I wonder if you have accommodations I might reserve for a few days?"

"So she wanted to rent a room? At Cedar Lodge?" Benjamin laughed.

"Well, you don't have to sound so incredulous," I snapped, jerking my hand free of his. "And what's so funny?"

We'd decided to go for a short walk around the neighborhood while we talked. It had been very nice up until now.

"Sorry, honey. It just struck me as funny that someone would come all the way from Germany and stay in Cedar Chapel in a boardinghouse for senior citizens. Especially with all the fancy hotels in Branson and Springfield."

"I know. I thought it was odd, too. But she didn't explain why she's coming. I can't help wondering if she's related to Trent Stewart."

"Why would you think that?"

"Oh. I still haven't told you."

"Told me what?"

By now we had arrived back at the lodge. We went up the steps and sat on the porch swing.

"Okay, promise you won't throw a fit."

"What have you been up to, Victoria?"

"Promise."

"Fine. I promise."

As I told him about the morning at Trent's cabin, his mouth tightened. My heart lurched. Surely he wasn't picking up on my guilt feelings, but true to his word, he didn't say anything.

"Okay, I know I told you I wouldn't do any more investigating without talking to you first. But Miss Simone was out of the house all afternoon. In fact, she's still not back." I shot him a look. "I couldn't resist the opportunity to check things out."

He groaned. "By check things out, I assume you mean you searched her rooms."

"Well, it was a good thing. You'll never believe what we found."

"We?" He looked puzzled.

"Miss Jane and Miss Georgina sort of found me there, so they helped."

"I see. All right, Vickie, I should know by now that you simply can't help yourself when an opportunity to search for clues arises. So what did you find?"

I'd folded the copy of the photo and crammed it into my jeans pocket before he'd arrived. Now, I produced it.

Surprise crossed his face as he looked at the photo. "Trent Stewart and Miss Simone?"

"Yep. That's who they are."

"Hmm. Looks like those hunches of yours are paying off." He smiled and squeezed my hand.

"So you don't think it's a coincidence they know each other and haven't mentioned it?"

"In a town the size of Cedar Chapel? Probably not. I'd say by now the whole town would know, unless they deliberately kept it a secret."

"That's just what I thought. What are we going to do about it, Benjamin?"

"Oh, so now it's 'we'." He grinned.

"Of course, it's we. It's always been we." I leaned over and planted a kiss on his lips then quickly retreated. Shouldn't get sidetracked.

"I'm sure you've got something up your sleeve, since you've had several hours to think about it, so spill it."

"Okay. I do have a couple of ideas," I admitted. "I think we need to find out about the picture Trent knocked over in his cabin. That must be significant, since he obviously didn't want me to see it. I'll bet it's a photo of Miss Simone."

"But you already have a photo tying them together. I don't see the point." Little furrows appeared between his eyes. I resisted smoothing them with my fingers.

"Yes, but you see, I can't confront her about that one because she'd know I was snooping in her things."

His lips quirked. "Okay, so we break into another person's home and snoop in his things so that Miss Simone doesn't find out you snooped in hers. That's not only immoral but also illegal. You do realize we could go to jail."

His words pierced like a knife. "Okay. You're right. We'll just have to figure out another way."

He smiled. "We'll think of something. But don't you think we should show the photos to the sheriff before we confront anyone?"

"And tell him I invaded Miss Simone's room? When he'd just love to have a reason to throw me in jail?"

"I doubt he'd do that, since it is your own house and Miss Simone's door was unlocked. So how do you suggest we find out about the photo in Trent's house?"

"I'll think of something."

"I'm sure you will."

"Benjamin!"

"Sorry." He smiled and kissed me on the cheek.

"All right," I said, laughing. "How about if I manage to get an invitation to his cabin again?"

I waited. And waited. He just looked at me. Finally, he cleared his throat.

"Yes, I'm sure that wouldn't be difficult for you."

I gave him a quick glance. Did he know something? I couldn't tell from the oh-so-innocent look on his face, but I'd bet. . .

"The whole town knows he's been coming on to you, Vickie." A muscle beside his mouth jumped. And I could see the question in his eyes. If only I could tell him I was totally innocent. As I hesitated, pain filled his eyes.

Shame washed over me. I blinked and ducked my head as a mist clouded my vision.

"I love you, Ben. Nothing happened. I promise."

I lifted my eyes to him, and suddenly, they flooded over.

He reached over and pulled me to him. "I thought I might be losing you."

"Never." I snuggled close to him. *Thank You, Father. Thank You for not letting me pull my life apart.* Suddenly, a picture filled my mind. I stood at the top of the grand staircase at Pennington House, wearing a lovely white wedding gown. Benjamin, handsome in a black tuxedo, stood waiting at the bottom of the stairs. A shiver ran through me. A Pennington House wedding. Could anything be more perfect?

He looked down at me and smiled. It was almost like he read my thoughts, but I knew that wasn't possible. Still, I couldn't prevent the blush I felt washing over my face.

"I think we'd better nix the idea of another visit to his cabin. Okay?"

"Okay, that probably wasn't a very good idea."

I heard the front door close softly and jerked my head around. No one was in sight. Had I imagined the sound?

Trent's face was shadowed in the darkened restaurant. His eyes seemed to glow for a moment, and to my imagination, they gave him a diabolical look. Funny how different he seemed to me tonight. He reached for the menu, and I shivered as his hand brushed mine. A very different kind of shiver than the ones I'd experienced in his presence before. *I never should have come here.*

"I was very pleasantly surprised when you called. I'd about given up, you know."

I took a deep breath. *Snap out of it, Victoria.*

I forced myself to smile. "Well, I decided there's nothing wrong with friends having dinner together. I really enjoyed our visit the day of the storm."

"So did I." His lazy smile bordered on seductive. A great deal more than friendly.

The waiter appeared at our table. "Would you like the wine list, sir?"

Trent raised his eyebrow, and when I shook my head, he waved the man away.

When I'd called him that morning, I wasn't expecting him to suggest Branson, although I should have known. Perkins' Café was as nice as you could get in Cedar Chapel, and Caffee Springs wasn't a lot better. But as I sat across from the man I suspected of murder, I found myself wishing I'd told Ben of my plan. The seniors were the only ones who knew I planned to get information out of Trent. Surprisingly, they hadn't even cautioned me against it.

Our drinks arrived, and we placed our food orders. I was sure he'd rather have something stronger than the ginger ale in front of him.

I took a long drink from the frosted water glass then set it on the table.

"It's wonderful to see you across from me. You're the most beautiful woman here, you know." He reached over and took my hand.

I didn't bother to blush or simper. I knew a line when I heard one.

I slipped my hand from his but not before he'd run his fingers across my ring.

"Engagement?" He asked, obviously disappointed.

I looked at the jeweled circle on my right hand and shook my head. "Actually, it's a friendship ring Benjamin gave me when I turned thirteen. I found it a couple of months ago. I'm surprised it still fits."

"But you did tell me you were engaged, didn't you?" he asked.

"Yes, although we haven't set a date. Yet."

"Ah, the foolish Benjamin takes his time."

"Actually, the foolish Victoria is the one who's been holding things up."

"I see. So you and this Benjamin have been close all your lives?"

I laughed. "Benjamin and I were friendly enemies when we were kids. But that was a long time ago."

Our food arrived. I picked at mine, unable to eat more than a few bites. I had no idea how to bring up the subject of Miss Simone.

"Do you have an appointment, or are you in a hurry for the evening to end?"

Now, how could I answer that without lying?

A ringing sound came from my evening bag. I reached inside and grabbed the cell phone Frank had crammed into my hand when he found out whom I was lunching with.

Miss Jane's breathless voice emitted from the phone. "Victoria, we have the evidence you and Ben wanted. Meet us back at the lodge as soon as possible."

21

With my heart in my throat, I managed to stay on the road during the thirty curving miles to Cedar Chapel. My tires squealed when I turned into the driveway at the lodge. Before I could unsnap my seat belt, Miss Jane was yanking my door open. I jumped out.

"Miss Jane, what have you been up to?"

"We went to Trent Stewart's house while you had him occupied. We didn't figure the sheriff would jail us for it. And we hit pay dirt." The triumphant look on her face told me they'd found something significant.

We rushed up the porch steps and into the house, where all the seniors except Miss Aggie surrounded us.

"Where's Miss Aggie?"

"Still at Pennington House," Frank said. "She's gonna be so mad she missed this."

Why hadn't I known they were up to something? A knot formed in my stomach. If Trent had caught them there, they could have been in big trouble at the least and possibly even great danger.

"Ben is on his way," Frank said with a pleased look on his face. "We figured we could show you both at the same time."

We flocked into the front parlor.

Before we could sit down, Ben's truck pulled up and he rushed in.

"What's going on? Victoria, I thought we agreed we wouldn't break into Trent's cabin."

I motioned to the seniors. "Wasn't me."

"It was us," Miss Georgina declared. "Jane overheard you and Victoria talking about the photo. She told the rest of us, and we decided to do a little breaking in ourselves if we had an opportunity."

"Yes," said Miss Jane, excitement erupting from her throat. "And when Victoria told us she was having lunch with Trent Stewart to dig for information, we decided it was the perfect time."

"And it was," Martin chortled, holding up a small digital camera.

I cringed as Ben stared at me, his lips tight. "You had lunch with Trent?"

"Don't look at me like that. It was the only thing I could think of. I knew if I told you, you'd try to stop me."

He took a deep breath. "We'll talk about it later. Right now, we need to look at Martin's photos."

Grateful for the reprieve, I was only too happy to follow his lead. As Martin scrolled through the photos, we looked on, our excitement growing at what we saw.

"I found this one on his nightstand. If it's the one he knocked over when you were there, he was pulling a fast one. As you can see, there's not a scratch on it."

I caught my breath. It was a photo of Trent in cap and gown, standing between Jack Riley and Miss Simone.

"Ben," I said softly, "do you think Trent could be Miss Simone's grandson?"

"If I was a betting man, I'd put my money on it."

"But why the secrecy? I don't understand." I sighed. "And what is Mr. Riley's place in this web?"

"Do you think he could be the grandfather?"

"Maybe, but all the rumors pointed to Forrest Pennington."

"Here, look at this one." Martin scrolled to the next picture.

I almost gasped as I looked. Trent, in cap and gown, stood next to a young girl, maybe seventeen. Her curly hair and quirky smile sent a chill down my arms.

"Benjamin! She's practically a female version of Corky."

"Yeah, I can see that," he said.

"She's a Pennington, Victoria. I'm almost certain," Miss Evalina said.

"I think so, too. Look at that hair."

"And her eyes, Victoria." Miss Jane's emotion-filled voice cracked. "She has Aggie's eyes."

"And her cheekbones." I ran my finger over the girl's face. "So, what do you want to do? Should we show these to Miss Aggie?"

"I don't know." Miss Jane's forehead wrinkled up with worry. "There's no telling what she'll do. You know how quickly she took Corky into her life. It's as if she was starved for family."

Thankfully, sweet, family-oriented Corky had turned out to be good for Miss Aggie, but what did we know about these people?

"What do you think, honey?" Ben's soft voice soothed my jumbled nerves.

"We have to. It's not fair to keep this from her." I sighed then glanced around at the seniors. "Did you find anything else?"

"Nothing significant. Apparently, these two photos were important enough to Trent for him to risk discovery if they were seen."

"Well, I'm waiting up for Miss Aggie," I said. "She has

a right to know about these photos as soon as possible."

"How about we connect the camera to your computer and get a printout while we wait?"

"Good idea, Ben. There's printer paper in the left-hand drawer."

The sound of a car pulling into the garage drew our attention.

"There's Aggie now." Miss Georgina wrung her hands. "I hope this news won't be too much of a shock to her."

A few minutes later, Miss Aggie sat in the parlor with Miss Jane on one side and Miss Evalina on the other.

Walking over to Miss Aggie's chair, I put my arm around her. Something I didn't usually do to the sometimes caustic lady.

"Could I speak to you alone?" I whispered.

Fear jumped into her eyes, and I hastened to reassure her. "Nothing's wrong."

"I'll be back," she announced to the others.

We went to my office, where we found Benjamin taking the sheet with the photos from the printer. He held it up.

Apparently, Miss Aggie's vision focused on the one of Trent with Miss Simone and Mr. Riley.

A sound of impatience came from her throat. "Why are you showing me these? We already know they know each other."

"Look at the other one, Miss Aggie." Ben adjusted the sheet.

Miss Aggie looked at the photo of Trent and the girl. A confused look crossed her face. She took it from Benjamin's hand and walked over closer to the desk lamp. She peered at it closely.

"The girl looks like my mother," she almost choked out. "Who is this? Where did you get it?"

"We don't know who she is, Miss Aggie, but we suspect she's a Pennington. We needed to know if you agreed."

"Well, I certainly do agree," she said. "I suppose Trent and this girl are Jenny's grandchildren, which pretty much proves Forrest really was the father of her child."

"Let's not jump to conclusions, Miss Aggie. There could be another explanation."

She looked at me with narrowed eyes. "Well, I'm getting to the bottom of this right now."

She stomped up the stairs with me hurrying after. At the top, she turned and stared at me. "I don't need your help, missy. You can just take yourself back down those stairs."

"Now, Miss Aggie. I'm sorry, but I can't let you confront Miss Simone alone. We don't know what she'll do."

"I can handle Jenny Simon, young lady."

"I'm sure you can. Nevertheless, if you insist on doing this, I'm going with you."

"Hmph. Fine." She turned and walked down the hall then pounded on the door to Miss Simone's suite. When there was no answer, she pounded again.

We heard footsteps crossing the room.

"Wh—what? Who is it?" Miss Simone's voice trembled. She'd probably been awakened from a sound sleep.

"It's Aggie. I want to talk to you."

"Well, for heaven's sake. Can't it wait until morning?"

"No, it can't wait until morning. Open the door. Right now."

I cringed. A little discretion would be nice, but discretion wasn't Miss Aggie's strong point. Especially when she was riled up.

A few moments later, we heard the bolt pulled back, and the door opened. Miss Simone, pale and obviously frightened, invited us in.

As soon as Miss Aggie's feet crossed the threshold into the sitting room, she thrust the photos in Miss Simone's face.

"I want to know who these people are," she demanded.

"Aggie, I can't see when you wave them in my face." Miss Simone snatched the photos away from Miss Aggie and walked to an overstuffed chair. Turning on the lamp, she leaned over and stared at the photos.

I heard her take a deep breath, then she sat in the chair and leaned back, covering her eyes with her free hand.

"Who is the girl, Jenny?" Miss Aggie snapped.

"Why don't you sit down, Aggie? You, too, Victoria."

We sat on a sofa across from her, and I watched emotions battle across her face.

"Who is she?" Miss Aggie asked again. But her voice had lost a little of its sharp edge.

"My granddaughter, Samantha." The pride in Miss Simone's voice was undeniable. "Where did you get the photo?"

"Who is her grandfather, Jenny?" Miss Aggie ignored Miss Simone's question.

Miss Simone licked her lips, and her eyes darted from Miss Aggie to me.

"Jack Riley."

A short laugh emitted from Miss Aggie's throat. "Try again. She looks just like my mother. You can't have missed that."

Miss Simone's face was a picture of surrender. She

took a deep breath then let it out slowly.

"Actually, Aggie," she said, "I've always thought she looked quite a bit like you when you were young. But then, you looked just like your mother."

I looked on in amazement as Miss Aggie's face was transformed. A radiance seemed to wash over her countenance.

"You really think so?" she whispered.

"Yes, Aggie. And it's true. Forrest was the father of my little girl, Helen. Samantha's mother."

Helen? Banks, perhaps?

"Why didn't you tell me? Why didn't you tell my parents they had a grandchild?"

"Because Forrest had chosen to marry someone else and denied the child was his. I wasn't about to go begging to the Pennington family."

"So where does Trent Stewart come into the picture?" I asked. "And Jack Riley, for that matter?"

Her face closed up as though she'd drawn a shade. "Jack Riley is my lifelong devoted friend. Trent Stewart is his protégé."

She stood up, and it was obvious she'd said as much as she intended to.

"Aggie, we'll talk tomorrow. Samantha found out about her Pennington connection recently, and I'm sure if you'd like to meet her, she would be thrilled. But that's up to you."

Miss Aggie nodded silently. I couldn't remember ever seeing her so speechless. She turned as we got to the door.

"Jenny," she said, "I'm so sorry. I always knew Forrest was no good. I wish I'd known. I wish I could have helped."

She stepped out into the hall before Miss Simone could answer then walked down to her room and slipped through the door.

⸻

When I got downstairs, I briefly told the rest about the exchange between the two women.

A cacophony of chattering broke out as the news sank in. I knew I needed to calm them down. Before I had a chance to speak, Frank cleared his throat.

"We have news again."

All eyes turned to him.

"Oh dear, please don't tell me you and Eva have changed your mind?" Miss Georgina was obviously distressed.

Frank grinned. "Don't know why you always think the worst. The fact is, we've decided on a date and a place. Or almost." He reached over and squeezed his fiancee's hand.

Miss Evalina smiled. "We'd like to have the ceremony here, Victoria, as I said before. Sometime next month, if that's satisfactory."

"Of course. Just let me know the date so we can plan for it."

"How 'bout the thirty-first?" Martin snickered.

"Martin, that's Halloween," Miss Georgina said with a frown. "Eva doesn't want to get married on Halloween."

"I'm sure Martin was just teasing, dear." Miss Evalina patted her cousin's plump shoulder and then glanced at me. "We were thinking around the middle of next month on a Sunday afternoon, if that can be arranged."

"Absolutely. It's no problem. We'll take a look at the calendar and start planning."

"I don't want a fuss." She smiled at Frank. "I should have said we don't want a fuss. Just a few close friends and Frank's son and his family."

"Where are you going on your honeymoon?" Martin said with a snicker.

"Martin." Miss Georgina's face flamed, and she wrung her hands.

"Sorry, Georgina." Martin appeared contrite. "I didn't mean to embarrass you."

She blushed and ducked her head.

"As a matter of fact, we're going to Florida," Frank said.

"Disney World?" Miss Jane asked.

"Among other things. Maybe we'll hang out at the beach, too."

"Well, be careful," Miss Georgina warned, with a shiver. "Watch out for sharks."

When the seniors had finally wound down and retired for the night, Benjamin and I returned to the porch swing.

"Whew. What an evening." I stretched and sighed with relief.

He stretched his arm out behind me. "So, what's bothering you? Miss Simone didn't really say anything we hadn't already figured out, did she?" he mused.

"Not really. I'm glad she revealed the truth to Miss Aggie. But I felt there was more. It seemed to me that she was holding something back. Maybe something important."

I leaned back against his arm and yawned, closing my eyes.

"I'd better go home before we scandalize the neighborhood by sleeping on the swing together all night." I felt his lips touch one of my eyelids then the other.

"Umm-hmm. Good night, Ben."

"I'm not leaving until you're safely inside with the door locked."

"Oh all right." I sat up and stretched again. "Good night."

From behind the lace curtain on the front door, I watched him leave, then I ducked into the kitchen to make sure everything was in top shape. Mabel always left the kitchen spotless, and I tried to make sure it was that way when she came to work in the morning.

I poured a glass of milk and carried it upstairs with me. My bed was calling me, but I sat on the sofa in my sitting room and picked up my Bible. It was still open to the chapter in Luke I'd been reading that morning. I remembered reading the parable of the sower. I found my place and read on about not hiding my light.

Luke 8:17: "For there is nothing hidden that will not be disclosed, and nothing concealed that will not be known or brought out into the open."

Wow. My heart began to race wildly, and my face felt hot. Could God actually be speaking to me through His Word, or was it simply coincidence? My grandparents had taught me that God cares about every little incident in our lives. But although I loved and trusted Him, did I really believe He would speak to me in such a specific manner?

I read the verse again then continued on to the end of the chapter. By now, I was wide-awake. I changed into pajamas and knelt by my bed, speaking to my Father about the incidents of the day, hoping to have another experience like the one with the Bible verse. Although no thunder sounded and no burning bush appeared, warmth and peace washed over me. I leaned my head on the bed and basked in the feeling for a while. Finally, I crawled between my soft, smooth sheets, inhaling the soothing scent of lavender.

⁓

"Victoria! Wake up!" I started and sat straight up. A loud pounding on my apartment door accompanied the shouting.

I jumped out of bed and ran to the door, flinging it open. Miss Jane stood with her arm raised, ready to knock again, and drew it back just in time to keep from hitting me in the face. I could hear doors opening on the second floor.

"Aggie's gone. She just took off in her car. I saw her." Miss Jane was breathing heavily, and I coaxed her inside and urged her to sit down on the sofa.

"Miss Jane, calm down. Tell me from the beginning. What happened?"

"I woke up to the sound of a car engine. Then, I heard the garage door opening. You know how it squeaks." She stopped and took a breath. "I looked out the window and saw Aggie's Lexus driving off down the street."

"Maybe someone stole her car." We both looked up to see Miss Georgina standing in the open doorway. The rest of the seniors stood behind her, peering into my suite.

"That's what I thought at first," Miss Jane said, "so I went to her room. She's not there. Where would she go this time of night?"

Miss Jane didn't get upset like this. It was usually Miss Georgina who went to pieces. But Miss Jane and Miss Aggie were lifelong best friends. And it hadn't been that long since Miss Jane thought she had lost her.

"All right, does anyone have an idea where she might have gone?"

Five heads, from steel gray to snow-white, shook in the negative.

"We'd better call the sheriff," Frank suggested.

"Let's call Corky first. Maybe he knows something." I picked up my phone and dialed Corky's cell. He answered on the fourth ring. Quickly, I told him the news.

"Have you tried her cell phone?"

"Oh, Corky, I forgot all about her new cell phone."

"Okay, I'll call her and get back with you."

A couple of minutes later, the phone rang.

It was Corky. "She's not answering. I'm coming over."

He hung up, and the seniors and I looked at each other helplessly.

"Let's get dressed and meet downstairs," I said. "And try not to worry. I'm sure it's something perfectly simple and Miss Aggie's fine.

"Oh no," Miss Georgina whimpered. "Aggie's missing again."

22

Well, I'm going to Pennington House." Miss Jane got up from the sofa and headed for the door. She hadn't calmed down much from the moment she'd seen Miss Aggie drive off.

"Miss Jane, wait." I started after her, and she stopped, throwing me an impatient look.

"Wait for what?" she retorted. "Can you think of anywhere else she'd have taken off to at this time of night?"

I stared, mentally slapping myself. Of course Miss Jane was right.

"Frank, will you call Corky and tell him to meet me at Pennington House? I'll call Benjamin." I yanked the receiver up from the hall phone and dialed Benjamin's number, surprised when he answered on the first ring.

"I'm on my way, Vickie. Corky called."

"No, no. Don't come here. Meet me at Pennington House. Whatever Miss Aggie's up to, she's probably there."

"All right, but stay in the van until I get there. Did anyone tell Corky about the change in plans?"

"Frank's calling him now."

I hung up the phone and turned to see the seniors waiting expectantly. Apparently they all planned to go with me. They all wore sweaters or jackets. How could I keep them from going along? If Miss Aggie had gone to Pennington House, she had a reason. Someone might have called her and asked them to meet them there. I couldn't believe she would have gone anywhere in the middle of the night otherwise.

Miss Simone came down the stairs, fully dressed. "Have you heard anything more yet?"

"No, but I'm meeting Benjamin and Corky at Pennington House. We think she might have gone there."

"That's what I thought when I heard she was gone. If you don't mind, I'd like to go, too." I looked in surprise at Miss Simone, who seldom wanted to be near us.

"And we're going," Frank stated, darting a challenging look at me.

I decided to try reasoning with them.

"But don't you think it would be best if you stayed here, just in case Miss Aggie should call or come home?"

"We're going, Victoria," Miss Jane said.

I knew there was no time to argue with them when they'd obviously made up their minds.

"All right. Let's go." We headed through the kitchen, where I grabbed a sweater off the rack by the door leading to the garage.

I jumped as a howl reverberated from beneath us.

Miss Georgina looked toward the basement door. "Maybe we should take Buster along."

She could be right. It wouldn't hurt to have the monster dog along, for morale if nothing else. I grabbed Buster's leash and let him out of the basement. He rushed past me and the leash, bounding after the seniors, through the garage door.

We crowded into the van. Buster jumped into the rear seat with Frank and Martin.

I headed down the street past the square and turned onto the blacktop highway that would take us to the Penningtons' private road.

Once we left town, the night was black, the only light

coming from the headlights.

"It's so dark and scary out here." Miss Georgina's trembling voice echoed from the seat behind me. "Do you really think Aggie would have driven here all alone?"

I tried to push the thought from my mind as my eyes peered into the shadowy darkness on the sides of the road.

"Aggie's not afraid of anything," Miss Jane stated. "Can't you go faster, Victoria?"

"I'm already over the speed limit. We're not going to be much help to Miss Aggie if we end up in a ditch."

"Move over, Buster!" Martin snarled. "And quit slobbering all over me."

"Really, Martin. I'm sure he understands every word you say." Miss Evalina, in the seat beside me, turned and scowled toward the back.

All our nerves seemed to be on edge. I hoped Benjamin or Corky would be at Pennington House when we got there, so we wouldn't have to wait in the van.

"There's the turn, Victoria." Miss Georgina leaned forward and pointed. I was about to sail right past it in the dark.

"Thank you, Miss Georgina, I see it." I slowed down and turned onto the dirt road.

"Be careful now. It's awfully steep, and there's a curve about halfway up."

"Be quiet, Georgina. She knows there's a curve. Leave her alone and let her drive." I cringed as Martin's voice rang out through the van.

"I—I'm sorry, Martin." Miss Georgina sniffled right behind my ear.

Martin cleared his throat. "Ah. . .well, I'm sorry, too." Wow! Martin apologizing?

"I wish you'd both stop your foolishness," Miss Evalina said. "We need to be thinking about Aggie right now."

We reached the top of the hill, and I stopped. Miss Aggie's Lexus was parked right behind Trent Stewart's SUV.

Pennington House loomed dark and foreboding behind them.

There was no sign of Benjamin or Corky.

"She's here. Just like we thought," Miss Georgina said, "but who does that little van belong to?"

"It's an SUV, not a van," Frank said.

A shiver ran through me. "That's Trent's SUV."

"Victoria, what should we do?" Miss Evalina glanced at me then at the SUV. "Aggie may be in trouble."

"How about you ladies stay in the car while Martin and I scout around?" Frank said, ever the protector.

"I think that's a good idea, but I'm going with you." I turned and looked at Miss Evalina then the other three ladies. "Please stay in the van until we know it's clear."

They complied, but by the mulish expressions on their faces, I knew they weren't happy about my order.

"I mean it," I said, looking at each one. They exchanged glances then stared at me with mutiny in their eyes. "I don't have time to argue. Stay with Buster. He'll keep you safe."

Frank, Martin, and I got out of the van and began to stealthily make our way toward the mansion.

"What if the door's locked?" Frank whispered.

"Did you forget I'm with you?" Martin said with a muted snicker. Martin's talents included lock picking.

"Shhh. They'll hear us," I whispered.

We tiptoed up the broad steps and crossed the porch to the heavy carved door. I looked at Frank and nodded. He reached over and turned the ornate doorknob. I closed my eyes and prayed, hoping that Corky had taken care of the squeaking hinges. The door opened smoothly without a creak.

Frank stepped cautiously through the doorway, with Martin on his heels. I was just about to step through when something bumped me from behind. I swung around, my fist raised.

Miss Jane raised her hand and caught mine, her eyes wide. Miss Evalina, Miss Georgina, and Miss Simone stood behind her. My breath hissed through my lips with exasperation, and I dropped my hand.

"I told you to stay in the van. I almost hit you. I could have hurt you."

"But you didn't," Miss Jane said, smiling sweetly. "We're probably safer with you anyway, than out in the dark alone in the van."

Really, was I any better? Hadn't Benjamin told me to stay in the van until he arrived? But I couldn't let Frank and Martin go inside alone, could I?

Miss Georgina held Buster's leash, and he squirmed and whimpered at the end of it. Somehow, it seemed he knew not to bark. I sighed. Why had I thought they'd stay in the van? I put my finger to my lips and turned and went through the door, with the ladies and Buster following close behind.

Frank and Martin stood in the wide foyer looking up the staircase. When they saw the women behind me, they didn't appear surprised at all. Frank pointed up the stairs. There was a light on somewhere on the second floor. A bolt of fear shot through me, and I struggled to push it away.

Frank started up the stairs. Swallowing, I tiptoed after him, my palm sliding upward on the banister. I crept, step by step, toward the second-floor landing. I could tell from the heavy breathing that my friends followed close behind. Frank stopped and waited for me, placing his hand on my elbow. Glad for his welcome presence beside me, I gave him a grateful smile, and we continued up the stairs side by side.

We stepped onto the landing and stopped. Buster scrambled up the last step and stood panting. Moonlight streamed through a small window high above us. It wasn't bright enough to be the light we searched for. The light was ahead of us, down the hallway. I turned and started down the plush carpeted hall, with Frank close beside me. The others followed.

This floor had been totally renovated. The smell of fresh paint and new carpet was almost overwhelming in the closed-in space.

Silently, we all padded down the hall toward the unknown. The light was streaming from an open door. Cautiously, I stepped forward. The room appeared to be empty. I stepped through, and something brushed against my arm.

I gasped and turned, hitting this way and that, and my hand caught fabric. Buster rammed my legs. Everyone else crowded around me to defend me as I clutched my attacker—a lacy curtain, hung over a tall stepladder. I'd brushed against it as I walked past. I put my hand to my chest and drew in a stabilizing breath to slow my heartbeat.

"Sorry, folks," I whispered. "It looks like one of the workers left the light on."

I faced my friends, knowing exactly what we needed to do. "The tunnel."

"Should have tried the tunnel from the beginning," Martin fumed as we left the room and hurried down the hall to the staircase.

"It was only logical to check out the light, Martin," Frank said.

We rushed as quietly as possible to the library. The bookcase had been swung out, and the door to the hall stood open. As we walked down the plush corridor, we began to hear muffled voices. I reached the opening to the secret room and stopped. The voices were louder now. And one was definitely Miss Aggie's.

"That's Aggie's voice," Miss Jane whispered. Before I could stop her, she pushed the door open.

Trent Stewart stood with his back to us. The gun in his hand pointed across the room at Jack Riley. The elderly man shielded Miss Aggie, who stood behind him. Miss Aggie's eyes widened as she saw us.

"I'm tired of listening to your lies. I want them now, or I start shooting." Trent waved the gun threateningly.

I stopped in my tracks, motioning the others back. Frank had come up behind me and peered over my shoulder. He tugged on my shirt and motioned me to back up.

Suddenly, Trent whirled and turned his gun our way. Shock crossed his face. Mr. Riley took a step toward him, but Trent swung the gun back in his direction.

"Don't try it, Jack. I'll shoot Aggie just right so she'll bleed to death. Slowly."

Jack pressed Aggie behind him. Trent smiled and backed up so he could keep us all in his sights. "Get in here, all of you. I won't hesitate to make someone suffer."

We obeyed.

"Over there, by them," he ordered, motioning toward Mr. Riley and Miss Aggie.

We crossed the room and joined the other two. I reached over and squeezed Miss Aggie's arm. Then I glanced at all my precious seniors. Once again, I'd led them into danger. Where was Ben? And Corky? Were they dead somewhere in the tunnel? Had Trent gotten rid of them and hidden their cars? And. . .I glanced around the room. Where was Buster?

"Well, well, the lovely Miss Storm. A shame to meet this way. You seem to show up every time I'm here. What? You didn't know it was me running into the woods the day you and your friend came snooping around?"

Miss Jane gasped and looked at me. So Trent was the one we'd interrupted that day. But why?

"Trent, what are you doing?" Miss Simone stepped forward, but when he pointed the pistol at her, she stepped back and stood by Jack, who touched her shoulder. "So, you're going to shoot us?"

Uncertainty crossed his face, but only for a fraction of a moment. His eyes narrowed.

"This isn't the way I wanted it. I tried to get you to join me."

"Join you in theft? And murder? Because you murdered that man they found in the tunnel, didn't you? And you poisoned Jack, too. The man who loves you like a son."

Trent flinched at the accusation, but he tightened his lips and didn't answer.

"That's what I thought," Miss Simone whispered.

Shock exploded in my head. Trent had poisoned Mr. Riley? But when and how?

Jack put his arm around Miss Simone, and she leaned against him.

"We had coffee together just before I went to Caffee Springs. You slipped it into my cup. Son, why?"

"You know why I'm doing this. I'm doing it for *her*."

"For her? How can you say that? Does Samantha know what you're up to?" Jack's scornful voice rang out in the room.

Trent sent a glance of hatred toward the older man. "You never thought I was good enough for Samantha. You never would have allowed us to be together. Even if I'd found the emeralds. That's why I had to get you out of my way."

My stomach churned. Was he insane? How could I have thought I was attracted to this man?

I glanced furtively around the room. There had to be something I could do to get us out of here. The tall, heavy paperweight on the desk next to me caught my eye. If I could reach it, I could throw it and knock the gun out of Trent's hand, but it was on the other end of the desk. Furtively, I tried a tiny step. Trent swung toward me. I stared back at him. He looked away, and I let out the breath I'd been holding.

Out of the corner of my eye, I saw a flash of movement in the corridor behind Trent. I caught my breath. Trent looked at me again. This time, he must have noticed something in my expression.

"What are you up to, Victoria?" He waved the gun at me as he spoke. He seemed about to lose it, and that could be good or bad. On the one hand, he might get careless and give us an opportunity to overcome him. Or. . .he might shoot someone.

"What? I'm standing here, while you hold a gun on me. What does it look like I'm doing?"

Anger twisted his face, and I hoped I hadn't overdone it. I decided I'd better try to avert the explosion that seemed very near the surface.

"Actually, I need to go to the ladies' room."

A confused look crossed his face. Apparently he hadn't considered this problem. I silently applauded myself.

"Don't play games with me." He turned his attention back to Jack.

"Oh dear." Miss Georgina cried faintly. She wobbled and fell against Martin.

"Georgina. What's wrong?" Martin steadied her and peered into her face, then he turned to Trent. "She needs to sit down. She's about to faint."

Trent stared at Miss Georgina, a look of near panic on his face. "All right. Take her over to the desk. She can sit there."

Martin helped her to the chair and leaned over her,

placing his hand on her forehead.

"Okay, get back over there." Trent motioned to Martin with the pistol, and reluctantly he returned to stand beside Frank.

I started as Miss Georgina fell forward across the desk, knocking the heavy paperweight over so it fell. . .closer to me. Trent glanced at her and then turned his attention back to Jack. Miss Georgina lay still, and I peered at her in concern. I'd only known her to faint once, and I'd always suspected that wasn't real.

"I have to check on Miss Georgina." Without thinking of possible consequences, I hurried around the desk.

"What are you doing?" Trent screamed. "Get back over here." Miss Georgina's face was looking away from Trent. I barely controlled a gasp as she opened her eyes and winked.

"Okay, okay, I just wanted to make sure she was okay." I scurried back over to the others.

Clever Miss Georgina. She'd seen me looking at the paperweight and had staged the whole thing to get it within my reach.

I glanced at the others with their worried looks.

"She'll be okay. She tends to have spells, you know."

Trent turned his attention back to Miss Aggie. I didn't know how much time we had before he decided to carry out his threat.

"All I want is the emeralds and the location of the buried treasure," he said.

"I'm telling you," Miss Aggie said, "I have no idea where the emeralds are. They disappeared the night my husband died. And I've never even heard of any treasure."

Keep talking, Miss Aggie. Keep his attention. I reached

my hand behind me, grasping for the paperweight. I stretched, and my hand finally wrapped around the cold iron. I swung forward and threw the paperweight at Trent's arm. At the same moment, a golden flash of hair and teeth launched itself through the door at Trent. He turned to face his attacker. The paperweight flew right past him and hit Buster. He fell to the floor, dazed and whimpering.

Before Trent could react, Frank, Jack, and Martin plunged toward him. He whirled and raised his gun just before they reached him.

His face was a mask of rage. We'd lost our chance to escape. And worse, now he would probably kill all of us with no hesitation.

As I frantically tried to figure out another way of escape, the door to the second tunnel flew open and Benjamin fell through, followed by Corky. Trent swung around to face the new threat. Martin flung himself on Trent's back. Frank grabbed the arm that held the gun. Jack knocked the gun from his hand. Buster rose up from the floor, shook himself, and grabbed Trent's leg in his massive jaws.

"I see I'm just in time," Ben said, meeting my gaze with a wry smile. "Anyone got a rope?"

"Martin, did you see what I did?" Miss Georgina sat up straight, her voice jumping with excitement. "I knocked over the paperweight so Victoria could reach it. Did I help catch the crook?"

Martin, who was busy searching for something to tie Trent's wrists with turned and grinned. "You sure did. You're one smart cookie."

I looked on in amazement, as well as amusement, at Miss Georgina's radiant face. Well, well. Things were getting more interesting all the time.

"Yes, Sheriff. Trent Stewart." I glanced at Corky, who was speaking into his cell phone. "Yes, he's being tied up now. That's right, Pennington House." He flipped the phone shut and put his arm around Miss Aggie.

"Do you think we'll ever get this show on the road, Corky? It seems as though Pennington House is destined for trouble."

"Now, Aunt Aggie. Never fear. God is here." He smacked a very noisy kiss on her cheek, and she giggled.

Good for you, Corky. Keep reminding her of that. She needs it to get through all this.

Jack Riley and Miss Simone stood across the room talking to each other. She was weeping softly in his arms.

"Well, Victoria. We wrapped that one up, didn't we?" Miss Jane threw me a saucy grin.

"Yep, that we did." I laughed. "Of course, we may have had a little bit of help."

"But we laid the groundwork," she insisted.

"Absolutely, although I still have a lot of questions. We don't really know everything that's going on here."

"But we know Trent Stewart committed the murder here at Pennington."

"It seems likely, yes." But who was the dead man? And why did he have to be killed? The two questions continued to swirl in my head. I also wondered how Trent knew about the emeralds. Had Jack told him? I glanced at him. That was another mystery. If Jack told Trent, then who told Jack Riley?

Sirens screamed in the distance then drew closer. Martin headed for the front door to lead the sheriff to us.

Bob Turner stormed into the room with Tom Lewis at his heels. "Okay, what's going on here?" He glanced at Corky. "Would you like to explain a little more fully why this man is tied up in your house?"

"Actually, this is my aunt's house, if you'll recall. I just work here." He stepped back and motioned for Miss Aggie to take over.

After giving Corky a look that promised a reprimand to follow, she turned to the sheriff.

"This writer man called my cell phone and got me to come out here under false pretenses. He told me Corky was injured. When I arrived, he pulled that gun on me and demanded to know where some valuable items were located. Then, Jack Riley showed up." She turned to Miss Simone. "He told me you had called him and told him to get out here and check on me. Thanks. If he hadn't shown up, I don't know what I'd have done. He tried to reason with this Stewart fellow, but the idiot just grew angrier and began to threaten us both if I didn't give him what he wanted. Which I couldn't do because I don't know where they are. Then my friends from the lodge arrived. I'm not quite sure how, but he was apprehended. Then Ben and Corky crashed through the door." She took a deep breath. "And that's all I know about the matter."

"Sheriff," I said, stepping forward, "I'm pretty sure Trent Stewart killed the man in the tunnel."

He turned a sour look on me. "Are you now? And why is that?" Couldn't the guy ever cut me some slack?

"Because there is more going on here than you realize. I don't know all the details. Perhaps you should talk to Mr. Riley and Miss Simone."

"All right." The sheriff's voice boomed in the small space. "I want every last one of you to follow me to the courthouse right now. Because I intend to get to the bottom of this."

Well, duh, wasn't that what I'd suggested? I knew better than to say what I was thinking, though. I always felt the sheriff was waiting for an excuse to throw me in jail.

Deputy Lewis hauled Trent out the door, and the sheriff followed. "Now get there fast. Don't make me come looking for you," he threw back over his shoulder.

I smiled at Ben as he walked toward me. My hero. He'd gotten here in the nick of time. Although, I had to admit, the three elderly guys hadn't done badly. All I'd done was knock out my dog. The dog who now stood loyally by my side with his head tucked under my hand.

"Victoria, Corky and I parked on the road behind the woods. When we saw what was going on in the secret room, we ducked back out and came through the cave into the other tunnel."

That was my Benjamin. He always knew what to do. I smiled at my hero. "Okay, we'll go ahead and meet you at the courthouse." I raised my lips to meet his and saw that his eyes were clouded with worry.

"You broke your promise," he said.

"I'm sorry. I couldn't let Frank and Martin go inside alone." I paused at the skepticism on his face. "Everything turned out okay."

He shook his head. "What about next time? Am I going to have to worry about you for the rest of our lives?"

"What makes you think there will be a next time?"

"There's always a next time, where you're concerned." His lips touched mine and then he left.

Was he right? It did seem as though trouble sought me out. But I knew that wasn't what he meant. He thought I was the one who sought out trouble.

Miss Simone rode with Jack, and the gang and I, including Miss Aggie, piled into the van. She was too keyed up to drive her car and decided to leave it for Corky to come get the next day. Buster scrambled over to the rear seat and deposited himself between Martin and Frank. "Good dog, Buster. Good dog." Huh? Good dog? I jerked my head around to make sure that was really Martin I heard praising Buster. Wow! It was. I grinned. It had taken awhile, but the wild and woolly stray who'd come into our lodge and our lives last year had finally won over the dog hater.

When we arrived at the sheriff's department, Tom Lewis instructed us to sit down and wait to be called. We sat and looked around at each other, hoping it wouldn't be long before the sheriff called us in. It was 2:00 a.m., and after the harrowing events we'd just been through, we were all about to fall over from exhaustion. Miss Simone and Jack joined us a few minutes later.

The sheriff's door finally opened, and he looked around the room. "Where are Ben and Corky?"

"They're on the way, Sheriff," Miss Aggie said, her voice weary and strained. "Their vehicles were parked back on the old logging road."

"All right." Once more, he surveyed the room, his eyes resting on Miss Jane. "Miss Brody, you can be first."

"What?" I cried, jumping up. "You're going to grill us one by one? We'll be here all night."

He peered at me through narrowed eyes. "You can have a nice cell to wait in, Victoria, if you'd like."

With a huff, I dropped back into the chair, while Miss Jane followed the sheriff out of the room.

"What in the world is he thinking?" Miss Georgina whined. "He should have had us come in tomorrow morning."

"I think Bob is trying to teach us a lesson," said Miss Evalina.

"You mean, to stay off his turf?" Martin asked.

"I would use less vulgar terms but, in essence, yes."

Corky and Benjamin came through the door. We explained the situation to them.

"You know what I've been wondering?" Miss Georgina rubbed the toe of one shoe against her other foot. "What were Bob and Tom doing here this time of night?"

Corky coughed and put his hand up. It didn't help. I could still see the grin. "Uh, I called Bob at his house. I guess he picked Tom up."

"Oh." She picked up a magazine and opened it. Bless her sweet heart.

Miss Jane was out of the office in ten minutes, and Miss Georgina was next.

When he'd spoken to everyone except Miss Simone and Jack, the sheriff told the rest of us to go home. No one moved.

He threw his hands up in the air and exhaled loudly. "Fine! Stay here all night for all I care." To my surprise, he called the last two in together.

We sat for nearly an hour before the door opened and they came out, looking drained and exhausted.

Without a word, we all got up and trooped out.

Miss Simone got into the van with us this time, and we drove back to the lodge. But I'd made up my mind. Tomorrow, I'd find out the truth.

⸻

There was a chill in the great hall in spite of the roaring fire in the enormous fireplace. I'd asked Jack, Corky, Phoebe, and Benjamin to join us for dinner. I don't think anyone thought it was merely a social occasion.

I looked around the room with interest at how everyone had paired off. It was no surprise to see Corky and Phoebe on the love seat. And we were all getting used to Frank and Miss Evalina being nearly inseparable. Miss Simone and Jack were seated next to each other on two antique wing chairs. I hoped before the night was over to have their story. Everyone kept darting furtive looks toward one of the fireplace sofas, where Miss Georgina and Martin sat side by side. Miss Georgina's face was pink as she listened to Martin telling some story about Jesse James. Benjamin and I were across the room from each other, but a glance from one to the other brought us together in spirit.

I scanned the room with my gaze. It stopped on Miss Jane, and she smiled at me. Sadly. No, it wasn't really sadness. But a certain wistfulness. Instinctively, I knew what she was thinking. What was she going to do should Miss Georgina get married, with Miss Aggie so busy with the new hotel? Miss Jane blinked and looked away, probably guessing I'd seen into her soul.

The room grew quiet, and I realized everyone was looking at me.

I took a deep breath and stood up. "I asked everyone here because in one way or another we're each involved with the crimes that have been committed at Pennington House."

Jack cleared his throat and stood up. "I know you want an explanation, and Jenny and I are ready and willing to give it to you."

This I wasn't expecting. I looked at him in surprise, nodded, and sat down.

Benjamin leaned forward, and his face held that ravenous reporter look. I grinned and turned my attention back to Jack, who had turned to his niece.

"Phoebe, some of the things you're going to hear may disappoint you. I know you think your old uncle is something of a hero, and I'm afraid that image will be tarnished. But you're a grown-up young woman now, and real life isn't like a fairy tale." His smile softened the words, and she lowered her eyes.

"I can't remember a time when I wasn't in love with Jenny Simon." His eyes softened as he looked at Miss Simone. "Of course, my actions when I was a boy didn't always indicate it. Especially the times I tied her braids together or dipped them in the inkwell."

I was immediately reminded of me and Benjamin. Fond amusement crossed Miss Simone's face, momentarily erasing the sadness that had taken up residence there the night before. I understood exactly how she felt.

"I think I must have been around twelve the first time I asked for her hand in marriage. And the first time she broke my heart." He chuckled then sobered.

"The last time she broke my heart was when she left Cedar Chapel. But the next part of our story is hers."

Expectancy ran through me as Miss Simone sat for a moment with her head down.

She looked up and smiled sadly at us. "Most of you know a part of what I'm going to tell you. Probably just enough to have things figured out all wrong. I think it only fair, with the things that have happened, that I tell you the truth. The way it really was and is. I especially feel a responsibility to you, Aggie." She swayed a little, and I got up and moved her chair over so she could sit while she talked to us.

"Thank you, Victoria. I need to apologize to you for disrupting your peaceful household. I know you've been disturbed by some of my actions." When I started to speak, she held her hand up. "Don't deny it."

"My mother was head housekeeper at Pennington Estate. I grew up there in a small but neat house on the property.

"I don't remember when I first fell in love with Forrest. He went away to college when I was still a child of maybe five or six, and I don't remember him ever speaking to me. Until the year I turned fifteen. When he was home for Christmas that year, he smiled at me. And I was lost in his smile." She threw an apologetic look at Jack, who smiled sadly.

"When I was sixteen, he took me out to a roadhouse. My very first. And when he brought me home, he gave me my first kiss. I fell head over heels in love with him. I kept waiting for him to ask me to marry him. Of course he never did. He was a twenty-nine-year-old man. He was only having fun with me. By this time, he was working for his mother's family in New York City. Why would he want a child for a wife? But I didn't realize that at the time. When I graduated high school, I packed my suitcase and went to New York. You see, I still thought he loved me."

Shame washed over her face, and I could see it was a struggle for her to continue.

"Of course, he didn't marry me. He set me up in a pretty little two-room apartment and visited me every night. At first. Then, it became two or three times a week. Finally, he told me he was getting married and couldn't afford to get found out.

"I was brokenhearted, humiliated, and most of all ashamed. But the worst was still to come. Two weeks later, I discovered I was expecting a child."

Jack stood up and walked over to her chair, placing his hand on her arm. "Let me take it from here."

"Shortly after Jenny left Cedar Chapel, my uncle, who had an import/export business in Berlin, asked me to come there as an apprentice. He had no heir and wanted to see if I could fill that position, as he was in poor health and only expected to live a few more years.

"After a few months, he sent me to New York City to obtain some items for a client. I knew from friends what the situation was with Jenny and Forrest. While I was there, I dropped by as often as possible. I don't know why I tortured myself so, but I didn't trust Forrest and wanted to keep an eye on Jenny. Just before I was to leave for Berlin, Jenny broke down and told me her predicament. I was livid with anger. I went to see Forrest and told him Jenny was pregnant. He laughed and said the baby wasn't his. I knocked him out cold."

He looked at Miss Simone, and when she nodded, he continued. "I decided it was time to propose again to my sweet Jenny. I knew she wasn't in love with me, but I wanted to take care of her and the child. Finally, she agreed. We married. I had to leave for Berlin right away. I told my uncle that I was married, and he made it possible for me to travel back and forth in order to care for Jenny then later our daughter, Helen." He smiled. "Because make no mistake, from the very beginning, she was mine."

Miss Simone reached up and patted his hand. "I'll tell the rest, dear."

She bit her lip before she spoke. "Jack wanted me to move to Berlin, but I had started acting some while I was with Forrest, thanks to some of his connections. I wasn't willing to give it up. Shortly afterward, the war started in Europe. Jack came back to New York City and helped me raise Helen. After the war, we separated. He moved back to Berlin, and I let him take Helen with him. When she grew up, he took her into the business. She married and had a daughter. Samantha, my granddaughter."

"But what about Trent Stewart?" I blurted.

Jack nodded. "Trent came to work for us as an apprentice when he was a lad of sixteen. His parents were both dead, and I had compassion for the boy. After a while, the affection I felt was like a father to a son. Unfortunately, he had some undesirable traits. I caught him stealing once, and he began to hang out at taverns, often coming home drunk. As Samantha grew older, he fell in love with her. An unrequited love, for she didn't care for his wild ways. He seemed obsessed with the idea he could win her love."

Still puzzled, I said, "I still don't understand. Where do the murder and the jewels come in?"

Miss Simone took up the story once more. "One day, when Forrest was drunk, he told me Robert and he had a plan to steal the emeralds. He also told me about the cave and the tunnel. Robert, however, died, and the emeralds disappeared. I was telling the story to Helen one day, and Trent overheard. He got it into his head that Samantha was being robbed of her rightful share of the Pennington estate and should at least have the emeralds to compensate. He became obsessed. When I found out he had come to Cedar Chapel, I followed him here."

"The sheriff told us Trent confessed to killing the man," Jack said. "He had found the cave opening, but when he went inside, he found a man, apparently a transient, holed up there. A fight broke out. Trent picked up a rock and hit him. He claims he only meant to knock him out. Then when he realized he was dead, he carried the body into the tunnel and left it there."

Miss Simone took a deep breath and sat up straight. "Poor Trent. He'll spend years in prison. And he'll never have the emeralds or Samantha."

Epilogue

Ben and I watched as the Lincoln, carrying Miss Simone, Helen, and Samantha to the airport pulled away from the curb, stirring up the red and gold leaves that were piled up there. It had been wonderful getting to know them, and they'd promised Miss Aggie to return for the grand opening of Pennington House. Miss Aggie had agreed to a trip to Germany in the spring. Jack was going with them as far as the St. Louis airport, but he was returning to Springfield to hire an attorney for Trent and see what he could do for him. He couldn't desert the young man he'd taken under his wing so long ago.

"Ben, did you know that Simon Pennington offered half of his inheritance to Helen? Of course, Forrest had gone through so much of his share it wouldn't have amounted to much."

"Wow. What did she say?"

"She said she wanted nothing from a father who didn't acknowledge her. Of course she doesn't need it anyway. I think she's very well off."

Ben grinned at me then looked around. "Where are all the seniors?"

"They said their good-byes earlier and left for the center. Except for Miss Aggie. I'm sure you know where she is."

He laughed. "Running things at Pennington House."

"Right. I half expect her to put on a hard hat one of these days."

"So they still don't know where the emeralds are."

"No. And they don't know what went on in the cave at Pennington House." I sighed. "I wonder if that mysterious mansion will ever reveal all its secrets."

"Maybe. Someday. And you'll probably be in the big middle of it." Benjamin cleared his throat. "Uh, honey, could we sit awhile? And talk?"

"Sure." I started to walk toward the swing.

"No, not there. Let's go to the parlor."

"Okay," I agreed, although I was a little surprised.

We went inside, and Benjamin poked at the fire, which was already flaming.

"Are you all right?"

He flung the poker down and grabbed me by my arms. "No, I'm not all right, Vickie."

"What's wrong?"

"Sweetheart, I've been waiting for nearly a year for you to set a date. You're driving me crazy. I'm not even sure you want to marry me. If you don't, just say so. But if you do, honey, can't we please."

"Christmas."

"Huh?"

"Christmas. We can get married on Christmas."

"Really? Christmas?" The look of joy on his face filled me with warmth until I realized he'd misunderstood.

"Oh, Ben, no, not this Christmas. I meant next year."

His face fell. "But that's over a year from now."

"Yes, but the time will go quickly. I promise. And just think. Pennington House will be open by then. Can you imagine anything more wonderful than a Christmas wedding at Pennington House?"

He brightened. "You really are excited about it, aren't you?"

"Of course. I've been dreaming of a Christmas wedding at Pennington."

"Well, why didn't you say so?"

"I was waiting for you to ask again. After all, I didn't want you to think I was being forward."

He made a choking sound and pulled me to him. "I love you, Vickie."

"And I love you, Ben. With all my heart."

He lowered his head, and I lifted my face. For a kiss that just about knocked my socks off.

Frances Devine lives among the lovely hills and valleys of southwest Missouri. Her desire to write began at age nine, when she read her first Bobbsey Twins book, but she fell in love with mysteries a year later when she discovered Nancy Drew.

You may correspond with this author by writing:
Frances Devine
Author Relations
PO Box 721
Uhrichsville, OH 44683